Praise for

THE SISTERS GRIMM SERIES

Today Show Kids Book Club Pick
New York Times Bestseller
Book Sense Pick
Oppenheim Toy Portfolio Platinum Award
Kirkus Reviews Best Fantasy Book
A *Real Simple* magazine "Must-Have"
New York Public Library 100 Titles for
   Reading and Sharing Selection

"Why didn't I think of *The Sisters Grimm?*
What a great concept!" —Jane Yolen

"A very fun series . . ." —*Chicago Parent*

★ "The twists and turns of the plot, the clever
humor, and the behind-the-scenes glimpses
of Everafters we think we know will appeal to
many readers." —*Kliatt,* starred review

ALSO BY MICHAEL BUCKLEY:

In the *Sisters Grimm* series:

In the *NERDS* series:

THE SISTERS GRIMM

· BOOK SIX ·

TALES FROM THE HOOD

MICHAEL BUCKLEY

PICTURES BY PETER FERGUSON

AMULET BOOKS

New York

The Library of Congress has cataloged the hardcover edition as follows:
Buckley, Michael.
Tales from the hood / by Michael Buckley ; illustrated by Peter Ferguson.
p. cm. — (Sisters Grimm ; bk. 6)
Summary: When a kangaroo court of Everafters, led by Judge Mad Hatter, tries Mr. Canis for his past crimes as the Big Bad Wolf, the Grimms seek evidence to save their friend, although Sabrina questions whether he should be saved.
ISBN 978-0-8109-9478-2 (Harry N. Abrams)
[1. Characters in literature—Fiction. 2. Trials—Fiction. 3. Sisters—Fiction. 4. Magic—Fiction. 5. Mystery and detective stories.] I. Ferguson, Peter, 1968– ill. II. Title.
PZ7.B882323Tal 2008
[Fic]—dc22
2008000962

Paperback ISBN 978-0-8109-8925-2

Originally published in hardcover by Amulet Books in 2008
Text copyright © 2008 Michael Buckley
Illustrations copyright © 2008 Peter Ferguson
Excerpt of *The Everafter War* copyright © 2009 Michael Buckley

Printed and bound in U.S.A.
10 9 8

Amulet Books are available at special discounts when purchased in quantity for premiums and promotions as well as fundraising or educational use. Special editions can also be created to specification. For details, contact specialsales@abramsbooks.com or the address below.

ABRAMS
THE ART OF BOOKS SINCE 1949
115 West 18th Street
New York, NY 10011
www.abramsbooks.com

For my friend Joe Deasy

Acknowledgments

In writing this book I have mined the work of many great writers and folklore collectors. Without their prolific imaginations, the Sisters Grimm could have never come to life.

I'd also like to thank my editor, Susan Van Metre, for her patience and support; Maggie Lehrman for her careful reading and excellent ideas; my wife, Alison Fargis, for her help with brainstorming and, of course, for being the best-looking literary agent in the world; Jason Wells for making me famous and for his tireless efforts to keep me that way; Joe Deasy for his friendship and laughter; my family and friends and everyone at Abrams, whose continued support keeps these books well written and well read.

THE SISTERS GRIMM

BOOK SIX

TALES FROM THE HOOD

SABRINA HAD NEVER FELT AS CONFIDENT *as she did at that moment. For the first time in a long time she wasn't worried about monsters, villains, or lunatics. She didn't fear surprise attacks or betrayal by people she trusted. In fact, she was eager for a confrontation. Let one of the Scarlet Hand's thugs try something and she would crush them into dust! Her body was strong. Her blood was hungry. She was a wrecking machine.*

She wanted to tell her sister how she felt. If only she could make Daphne understand that what was happening was a good thing, but the words were hard to find. Her thoughts were cloudy and complicated. It didn't help that everyone was shouting, and the room was filled with strong winds.

Sabrina turned to Daphne. The little girl was undergoing her own transformation. A swirling black fog circled her body, blocking out most of her face. All Sabrina could see were her eyes, like two brilliant suns illuminating dark corners and obliterating shadows.

"Sabrina, you have to stop this!" Granny Relda cried.

Sabrina was confused. What did her grandmother mean? She wasn't doing anything wrong.

"You have to fight this!" Daphne said from behind the black fog. "I know you are still in there. Don't let him control you!"

"Why are you talking to me like this?" Sabrina asked. When no one replied, she realized her words were only in her head.

"Fight him, child," a voice said from below. Sabrina glanced down. Mr. Canis lay at her feet—old and withered, his body trapped in the clutches of a huge, fur-covered paw. It was squeezing the life from the old man's chest. She cried out, hoping someone would help her pull her friend from the monster's terrible grip, but her pleas ceased when she realized the claws that were killing Mr. Canis were her own.

1

FIVE DAYS EARLIER

abrina Grimm awoke with a crazy dream fresh in her mind. In it, she was walking along a stone path when she realized she was naked. She screamed and rushed to some bushes to hide herself, wondering how she could have left the house without remembering to get dressed. A moment later the worst possible person came along—Puck. Since she had little alternative, she begged him to bring her clothes. He flew off and quickly returned with a pair of jeans, a shirt, and sneakers, which he left by the bushes so she could dress in private. Then, surprisingly, he walked away without a single smart-aleck comment. Relieved, she put the clothing on and continued on her way, only to find people pointing at her and staring. She looked down and found she was naked, again. Puck appeared once more. He told her that clothes couldn't hide who she really was. That's when she woke up, angry and embarrassed. Even in her dreams, Puck was a pain.

She lay in bed, enjoying the cool breeze drifting through her bedroom window. The model airplanes hanging from the ceiling swayed back and forth. She watched them for a while, imagining her father building them when he was her age. He had put a lot of effort into the models. They were painted, glued, and assembled perfectly. Her father was meticulous.

Her little sister, Daphne, lay asleep beside her, breathing softly into her pillow. Sabrina glanced over at the alarm clock that sat on a night table next to her bed: 3:00 a.m. It was a good time, she thought. There were no emergencies to deal with, no impending chaos, no responsibilities, and, best of all, no prying eyes. She climbed out of bed, rushed to the desk sitting in the corner of the room, and opened the drawer. Tucked in the back was a little black bag. She snatched it up and tiptoed into the hallway.

Once she was in the bathroom, she flipped on the light and closed the door. It was nice for once to have the bathroom to herself. There were a lot of people living in the big old house in addition to Sabrina and Daphne: Uncle Jake, Granny Relda, Puck, and of course Elvis, the family dog, who often used the toilet as a drinking fountain. And they all shared one tiny bathroom. The line was long and privacy was in short supply.

Sabrina unzipped the little black bag, revealing a personal treasure trove of makeup: tubes of lipstick and lip gloss, eye shadow, mascara, blush, and foundation, as well as a variety of barrettes she had purchased with her allowance at a local drugstore. She dug her hands into the bag and went to work.

First she tried to apply the foundation, but it made her look like a ghost. Then, she accidentally put on too much blush, giving her a look of perpetual embarrassment. The mascara was thick and gloppy, and combined with the eyeliner, it made her look like an angry raccoon. The lipstick was fire-engine red.

When she was finished, she studied herself in the mirror and nearly cried. She looked like the joker from a stack of playing cards. She was hideous and worse, hopeless. She would never learn to use this stuff. Frustrated, she washed it all off. It was times like this when Sabrina especially missed her mother.

Lately, Sabrina's appearance had become more and more important to her. Though she didn't fully understand the changes she was going through, she knew they had something to do with growing up. It seemed like yesterday when she couldn't have cared less about what she looked like, but now she spent hours contemplating hairstyles. She gave serious consideration to whether her shoes matched her tops. It seemed as if all she could think about was how others might see her, and she hated herself for it. She had always detested girlie-girls, with their little dresses and hair in ribbons. They were so stupid and superficial. Unfortunately, she could feel herself becoming one of those girls. Each time she applied her lip gloss, she imagined another fleet of brain cells dying a horrible death.

Luckily, no one in her family had noticed her preoccupation with vanity—most importantly Puck. If he discovered she was visiting the bathroom in the middle of the night to primp and study her flaws, he would make fun of her until she was old and gray.

Abandoning her beauty regimen for the night, she washed her face and was about to shut off the light and go back to bed when she heard something bubbling in the toilet. The lid was down and she couldn't see what was causing the noise, but she had her suspicions. Before Puck moved in with the family, he had lived in the woods for a decade. So modern conveniences mesmerized him—none more so than the toilet. He loved to flush it over and over and watch the water swirl down the hole and disappear. For months he was convinced that toilets were some kind of magic, until Uncle Jake explained how indoor plumbing worked. Unfortunately, this knowledge only increased Puck's interest, and it wasn't long before he was conducting what he called "scientific research" to discover what could be flushed down the tubes. It started out with a little loose change, but the items quickly grew in size: marbles, wristwatches, doorknobs, balls of yarn, even scoops of butter pecan ice cream swirled and disappeared. Granny finally put an end to it all when she caught Puck trying to flush a beaver he had trapped by the river. Ever since, the toilet had been coughing up Puck's "experiments." Last week Sabrina found one of her mittens inside. Now, apparently, something else was making its way to the surface. She bent down and lifted the lid, hoping it was the missing television remote control, which had vanished months ago.

But it wasn't the remote control. Instead it was something so shocking she would have nightmares about it the rest of her life and an unnatural fear of toilets in general. Who would expect to lift the toilet lid and find a little man sitting inside?

"Who goes there?" he said in a squeaky voice. He was no more than a foot tall and wore a tiny green suit, a green bowler hat, and shiny black shoes with bright brass buckles. His long red beard dipped into the toilet water.

Sabrina shrieked and slammed the toilet lid down on the creature's head. The little man groaned and shouted a few angry curses, but Sabrina didn't stick around to hear them. She was

already running down the hallway, screaming for her grand-mother.

Granny Relda stumbled out of her room. She was wearing an ankle-length nightgown and a sleeping cap that hid her gray hair. She looked the picture of the perfect grandmother, except, of course, for the sharpened battle-ax she held in her hand.

"*Liebling!*" her grandmother cried in a light German accent. *Liebling* was the German word for *sweetheart*. "What is going on?"

"There's a person in the toilet!" Sabrina said.

"A what?"

Before she could answer, Uncle Jake came out of a room at the end of the hall. He was fully dressed in jeans, leather boots, and a long overcoat with hundreds of little pockets sewn into it. He looked exhausted and in dire need of a shave. "What's all the hubbub about?"

"Sabrina says she saw something in the toilet," Granny Relda explained.

"I swear I flushed," Uncle Jake said as he threw up his hands.

"Not that! A person!" Sabrina shouted. "He spoke to me."

"Mom, you've really got to cut back on all the spicy food you've been feeding the girls," Uncle Jake said. "It's giving them bad dreams."

"It wasn't a dream!" Sabrina cried.

Daphne entered the hallway, dragging her blanket behind her. She rubbed the sleep from her eyes with her free hand and looked around grumpily. "Can't a person get some shut-eye around here?"

"Sabrina had a bad dream," Granny Relda explained.

"I did not!"

"She says she saw something in the toilet," Uncle Jake said.

"I swear I flushed," Daphne said.

"Ugh! I'll show you!" Sabrina said as she pulled her grand-mother into the bathroom. She pointed at the toilet, then took a step back. "It's in there!"

Granny set her battle-ax on the floor and smiled. "Honestly, Sabrina, I think you're a little old to be scared of the boogeyman."

The old woman lifted the toilet lid. There was the little man, rub-bing a red knot on the top of his head and glaring at the crowd.

"What's the big idea?" he growled.

Startled, Granny slammed the lid down just as Sabrina had done. Sabrina, Daphne, and even Uncle Jake cried out in fright and backed out of the bathroom.

"Now do you believe me?" Sabrina said.

"Oh, my!" Granny cried. "I'll never doubt you again!"

"What should we do, Mom?" Uncle Jake asked the old woman.

"Elvis!" Granny Relda shouted.

Seconds later an enormous blur of brown fur barreled up the stairs, knocking a few pictures off the wall as it stampeded into the bathroom and came to a screeching halt. Only then could Sabrina see him properly: Elvis, the family's two-hundred-pound Great Dane. He barked at the toilet fiercely, snarling and snapping at the lid.

"Get him, boy!" Daphne ordered.

"You better surrender!" Uncle Jake shouted at the toilet. "Our dog is very hungry!"

Just then, another door opened down the hall and a shaggy-haired boy in cloud-covered pajamas stepped into the hallway. He scratched his armpit and let out a tremendous belch. "What's all the racket out here?"

"There's something horrible in the toilet!" Daphne shouted.

"Yeah, I think I forgot to flush," Puck said.

"Not that! A little man," Granny Relda said.

"Oh," Puck said. "That's just Seamus."

"And who is Seamus?" Sabrina demanded.

"He's part of your new security detail. Now that Mr. Canis is in jail, the house needs looking after, and to be honest, I'm too busy to do it myself. So I hired you all a team of bodyguards."

"Why is he in the toilet?" Uncle Jake pressed.

"Well, duh! He's guarding it, of course."

"Whatever for?" Granny asked.

"The toilet is a vulnerable entrance into this house," Puck explained. "Anything could crawl up the pipes and take a bite out of your—"

"We get the idea," Granny Relda interrupted. "What are we going to do when we need to use it?"

"Seamus takes regular breaks and has lunch every day at noon," Puck said.

"This is ridiculous," Sabrina said. "We don't need bodyguards and we don't need you to put some freak in the toilet!"

Puck frowned. "You should really watch who you're calling a freak. He's a leprechaun."

Seamus lifted the lid and crawled out of the toilet. He now had two purple lumps on his head and an angry look in his eyes. "I didn't sign on for this abuse, Puck. I quit!"

"Quit? You can't quit," Puck said. "Who will I get to replace you?"

"Go find a toilet elf. What do I care?" the leprechaun shouted as he stomped down the hall and between the legs of Uncle Jake, leaving a trail of little wet footprints behind him.

Puck frowned and turned back to Sabrina. "Now look what you've done—you've made Seamus quit! Do you know how hard it is to find someone to sit in a toilet all night?"

"How many more leprechauns are in the house?" Daphne asked, peering behind the shower curtain.

"That was the only one," Puck said.

"Good!" Sabrina said, relieved.

"But there's about a dozen trolls, some goblins, a few elves and brownies, and a chupacabra staking out the other vulnerable areas of the house."

Sabrina gasped. "There are freaks all over the house?"

"Again, *freak* is a really ugly term. It highlights how ignorant you are. This is the twenty-first century, you know," Puck replied.

Sabrina clenched her fist. "I'm going to highlight your mouth, pal."

"Give it your best shot!" Puck shouted. "Wait a minute. What's that on your lips?"

Sabrina quickly wiped her mouth on her sleeve, leaving a lipstick stain on her shirt. She quietly cursed herself for not washing well. "Nothing," she said sheepishly.

"Puck, we appreciate you looking after us," Granny said, stepping between Sabrina and Puck. "I know Mr. Canis would feel better knowing you are taking over his duties. I guess it can't hurt to have a 'security detail' around the house, but perhaps the bathroom might be the one place we don't need an extra set of eyes."

"Suit yourself, but if a dragon crawls up the pipes and toasts your rear ends, don't come crying to me," Puck said with a snort and headed back to his room.

Daphne peered into the toilet. "Could a dragon really fit in here?"

Granny Relda assured the little girl that her rear end was safe from dragon attacks. She praised Elvis for his bravery and scratched him behind his big ears, then encouraged everyone to go back to bed. "We're going to visit Mr. Canis bright and early tomorrow," she reminded them.

Another wasted trip, Sabrina thought to herself.

Granny, with Elvis trotting behind her, returned to her room, leaving Sabrina and Daphne alone with their uncle.

"Have you been up all night?" Daphne asked him.

Uncle Jake rubbed his bloodshot eyes. "Want to see where she is?"

"Absolutely," Sabrina replied.

The girls followed him back down the hall to the door to the spare bedroom. The room was sparsely furnished, with only a full-length mirror against the far wall and a queen-size bed in the middle. Lying on the bed were Henry and Veronica Grimm, Sabrina and Daphne's parents, who were currently the victims of a spell that kept them sound asleep. Nothing Sabrina and her family had tried could wake them up. They were like two Sleeping Beauties, only one of them needed a shave. Recently, there had been a glimmer of hope for the sleeping Grimms— a woman from Henry's past who might be able to right the family's tragedy. Uncle Jake had been keeping a close watch on her via one of the Grimms' most valuable magical possessions— a magic mirror.

Mirror wasn't exactly the best word to describe what it was. Mirrors reflect back what is in front of them, but this mirror was reflecting something else—or rather, some*where* else. Gazing into the silvery surface, Sabrina saw a beautiful curly-haired woman with a round face and green eyes. She had a splash of freckles on her button nose and her blond hair looked like precious gold against the bright blue sky. She was wearing a billowy white dress and sitting atop a camel. There were other people with her, each also on a camel, and they were snapping pictures of an ancient pyramid standing in a rocky desert.

"Goldilocks," Sabrina whispered to herself.

"It looks hot," Daphne said as she peered into the mirror.

"I think she's somewhere in Egypt. It's hard to tell exactly where, though. The place is overrun with pyramids," Uncle Jake said as he knocked on the edge of the mirror. "If this thing had sound I might be able to make out her tour guide's dialect."

"Last week she was in the Serengeti, the week before—South Africa. Why does she keep moving around so much?" Daphne said.

"Who knows?" Sabrina complained. "She's never in one place more than a few days and then she's jetting off somewhere completely different! How are we going to get a message to her? She's got to come back here. She's got to help us wake up Mom and Dad!"

Daphne and Uncle Jake seemed taken aback by Sabrina's sudden temper, but she felt she had a right to be angry. At one time their search to find a way to break the spell on her parents had seemed hopeless. Now that they knew this woman had the solution it was almost harder than before, as they had to watch her dart around the world on a silly vacation.

"Be patient, 'Brina," Uncle Jake said to calm her. "We'll track her down."

As if on cue, the image faded in the mirror, and in its place, a fierce, bulbous head appeared floating in the silver surface. He had strong features and thick lips and his eyes were as black as midnight.

"Hello, Mirror," Sabrina said.

"Hello, girls," Mirror said. "Could the two of you drag your uncle out of here? He's been lurking around this room for two weeks. He needs something to eat, and if you ask me he's long overdue for a bath."

"He's right," Daphne said to her uncle. "No offense, but you are getting a little rank."

Uncle Jake shrugged and threw up his hands in surrender. "Fine, I can start up again in the morning."

"After a bath," Mirror repeated.

Uncle Jake turned to the girls. "You two should run off to bed as well. You've got a big day tomorrow."

"More sitting outside the jail, hoping they will let us in to see Mr. Canis," Sabrina muttered. "It's a waste of time. Sheriff Nottingham won't let us in. We could be using the time to find Goldilocks."

"You may not see Canis, but I'm sure he appreciates the effort, Sabrina. What if you gave up on the day Nottingham had a change of heart?"

"You have to have a heart to change it," Sabrina grumbled.

"Are you coming with us?" Daphne asked her uncle.

"Not this time, peanut. I've got plans with Briar Rose."

"Another day of holding hands and smooching?" Daphne asked.

Uncle Jake smiled. "If I play my cards right."

• • •

Breakfast was never a pleasant experience for Sabrina. Granny Relda's cooking left a lot to be desired. Many of her signature dishes included roots and grubs, flowers and weeds, milk from unusual animals, and tree bark, all in heavy, bubbling sauces. But that morning her appetite was ruined not by her grandmother's culinary disasters but by a pig-snouted creature sitting on the table like an ugly centerpiece. It had beady red eyes, enormous blisters all over its face, and a long, blue forked tail it used to swat the flies that circled its melon-shaped head.

"I suppose you're part of the security team," Sabrina said to the creature.

It nodded and puffed up its chest proudly. "I'm a poison sniffer, I am. My job is to sniff out anything that might kill ya before you put it in your gob, if it pleases you, miss."

"My gob?"

"Your pie-hole, your chowder box, your mouth," it said as it wiped its runny nose on its hairy arm. "I'm going to take a snort of every bite. Puck's orders."

"Lovely," Sabrina said sarcastically.

Granny rushed into the room carrying a sizzling pan and a spatula. She flipped something that looked like a pink burrito onto Sabrina's plate.

"What is this?" Sabrina asked as she poked at her breakfast. She was sure that if she poked hard enough it would squeal.

"It's gristle and ham wrapped around heavy whipping cream. People love this in the Czech Republic," Granny said as she rushed back into the kitchen.

"People must be very unhappy in the Czech Republic if this is what they love to eat," Sabrina said. She leaned over to smell her breakfast, then eyed the ugly creature. "I'll give you five bucks if you tell my grandmother this is poisoned."

The creature shook its head. "I cannot be bought."

Granny rushed back into the room with a pitcher and poured some glowing red juice into Sabrina's glass.

"Your sister has something planned for all of us," the old woman said, gesturing at Daphne's empty chair. "She told me that today she is going to be a totally different person."

"She's going to start eating with a fork?" Sabrina asked.

"Don't tease her. She's got it into her head that she needs to grow up. When she comes down, try to treat her like an adult," the widow said.

Sabrina cocked an eyebrow. "You're kidding me, right?"

Just then, Daphne stepped into the room. Sabrina turned to face her and nearly fell out of her chair. Gone were the goofy

T-shirts covered with puppets and cartoons, the blue-jean overalls, the mismatched socks. Daphne was wearing a blue dress Granny had bought Sabrina for special occasions. Her hair was combed straight rather than in her usual ratty pigtails, exactly the way Sabrina wore her own hair. Plus, the little girl was wearing lip gloss. She sat at the table, placed her napkin in her lap, and nodded at her sister and grandmother. "I hope everyone slept well."

It was several moments before Sabrina realized her jaw was hanging open. "Is this some kind of joke?" she cried.

Daphne frowned, as did Granny Relda.

"Does it look like a joke?" Daphne snapped, then did something that made Sabrina's blood boil. Daphne turned to her grandmother and rolled her eyes impatiently. How dare she?

"So, I hear we have some appointments this morning, Grandmother," Daphne said.

Granny chuckled but managed not to burst into laughter. "Yes, indeed. I need the two of you to hurry with breakfast. We're going downtown."

"How?" Daphne said. "Uncle Jacob is spending the day with Briar."

"Good question. We all know it's a federal offense for you to get behind the wheel of a car," Sabrina said to her grandmother.

"And if you think we're getting into Rip Van Winkle's cab again you've lost your mind." She shuddered, recalling the hair-raising ride with the narcoleptic taxi driver.

"Oh, no. We're taking the flying carpet," Granny explained.

"Sweet! I call shotgun!" Daphne cried, but then quickly controlled herself. "I mean, that will be pleasant."

Then it was Sabrina's turn to roll her eyes.

After breakfast, Sabrina, Daphne, Granny Relda, and the odd food-tasting creature (who insisted on coming along as protection) sailed over Ferryport Landing aboard Aladdin's flying carpet. The carpet was just one of a number of magical items the family possessed. Sabrina's first experience riding the enchanted rug had nearly given her a heart attack, but Granny seemed to have more experience steering it and the trip went without incident.

Along the way, Sabrina gazed down at the town. Everything was changing. Once-thriving neighborhoods had been abandoned, and many homes were facing the wrecking ball. In their place, odd buildings were erected—castles surrounded by alligator-infested moats, mansions made from gingerbread and candy. Mr. Applebee's farm, the site of their first detective case, had been bought and converted into a gigantic chessboard reminiscent of Lewis Carroll's *Through the Looking-Glass*. The changes made Sabrina uncomfortable. They reminded her that she and her family were the only humans left in town.

Sabrina's world hadn't always been so bizarre. Long before magic mirrors, flying carpet rides, and toilet leprechauns, the Grimm sisters had lived normal, quiet lives in New York City. When their parents disappeared they bounced from one foster family to the next, eventually landing in the home of their real-life grandmother, who lived in a sleepy river town called Ferryport Landing. Sabrina remembered the day she and Daphne came into town by train. Ferryport Landing seemed like the most boring place in the world. But it had a shocking secret: Ferryport Landing was a settlement for fairy-tale characters, founded by her great-great-great-great-great grandfather, Wilhelm Grimm, one of the world-famous Brothers Grimm.

Sabrina guessed that most kids would love living among their favorite fairy-tale characters. Knowing Snow White lived down the street or that the Little Mermaid was swimming in the river might be a dream come true for some, but to Sabrina it was more like a nightmare. Most of the fairy-tale folks, who now called themselves Everafters, despised her family. The root of their hatred lay with Wilhelm, who, with the help of a decrepit old witch named Baba Yaga, constructed a magical boundary around the town to prevent a band of rebel Everafters from attacking nearby communities. The end result was "the barrier"—an invisible prison that trapped the bad Everafters, as well as the good, in Ferryport Landing forever. Naturally, the townsfolk were bitter, but they failed to realize that Sabrina and her family were stuck in the town, too. The spell would be broken if the Grimms died or abandoned Ferryport Landing, but with the steady stream of outlandish crimes to solve and the rogues' gallery of monsters, lunatics, and evil witches to combat, Wilhelm's descendents weren't going anywhere.

Lately, Everafter resentment of the Grimms was at an all-time high. Most of the bad feeling was fueled by the town's new mayor, the Queen of Hearts. Mayor Heart and her notorious Sheriff Nottingham had made it all too clear that humans, especially the Grimm family, were not welcome in Ferryport Landing. They raised property taxes so high that they were impossible for most people to pay. Humans were forced to abandon their homes and leave town.

When Granny and the family managed to scrape together the money for the tax bill, Heart and Nottingham tried another approach to rid themselves of the Grimms. They arrested the family's protector, Mr. Canis. Canis, who happened to be the Big Bad Wolf, was dragged off to jail as the sheriff, mayor, and dozens more Everafters—some the family had considered friends—revealed themselves to be members of a shadowy group known as the Scarlet Hand. The Hand wanted nothing short of world domination, and they were also responsible for much of the family's grief. Led by the still mysterious "Master," they committed dozens of bizarre crimes, including the kidnapping and spellbinding of Sabrina and Daphne's parents. Staying one step ahead of the Hand was a full-time job, one Sabrina's grandmother had undertaken with the help of Mr. Canis. And now they needed to find a way to get him back.

"There's Main Street!" Daphne shouted above the wind.

Seconds later, the flying carpet gently touched down outside an office building on the edge of town. Once everyone had stepped onto the sidewalk, the rug neatly rolled itself up, and Daphne hoisted it onto her shoulder.

"Wait here," the pig-snouted creature said. "I'll scout the neighborhood. It's best to stay out of sight. There could be snipers in the trees."

"I'm sure there are no snipers—" Granny started, but the little monster raced off before she could finish.

Sabrina and her sister followed the old woman down Main Street. It was particularly lonely that day. Many of the little shops that lined the street were shuttered and closed. The sidewalks were empty and the roadway clear of cars. The town's one and only traffic light had burned out. As far as Sabrina knew, Ferryport Landing had never been a bustling center of commerce, but there had been a time not so long ago when its little stores were filled with customers. Now most were abandoned. Signs hung in windows declaring EMERGENCY LIQUIDATIONS and AFTER 150 YEARS IN BUSINESS WE'RE CLOSING OUR DOORS. Those that weren't shut had a much more ominous sign in their windows: a bloodred handprint, the mark of the Scarlet Hand. One now hung on the door of Old King Cole's Restaurant.

"Looks like they got to him, too," Sabrina said, pointing out the sign.

"We're running out of places to eat in this town," Daphne grumbled. Normally, Daphne's single-minded obsession with eating would have made Sabrina smile, but the little girl was making a troubling point. The town was closing its doors to humans and any Everafters who didn't join the Scarlet Hand.

Eventually the family stopped outside of a small office building with huge picture windows and a manicured lawn.

"What are we doing here?" Sabrina asked. "I thought we were going to the jail."

"I don't think visiting the jail is a good use of our time," Granny said. "Nottingham has been most uncooperative. We haven't seen Mr. Canis in a month, and it doesn't look like things are going to change. I've decided to hire someone who can help us."

"We're going to meet an Everafter, aren't we?" Sabrina said, looking at her sister. She knew that Daphne usually couldn't resist meeting fairy-tale characters. She was known to squeal with delight and bite her hand when in the presence of one. "I guess it won't be such a big deal now that you're a grown-up."

"No big deal at all," Daphne said, quite seriously.

When their security guard returned and informed them that they were safe from snipers, the group went inside and climbed the stairs to the third floor of the building. There they found a single door with a sign next to it that read THE SHERWOOD GROUP: ATTORNEYS AT LAW. Sabrina scanned her memory for the name Sherwood, but nothing came to mind.

Granny opened the door to the office and ushered the girls inside. There they found themselves in the middle of a chaotic battle. Sabrina saw a number of men wearing business suits, but they were acting far from professional. They were sword-fighting, arm-wrestling, drinking beer from tall ceramic cups, and singing a rambling English tune as loudly as possible. The lyrics seemed to be about fighting or stealing or combinations of both, and once one song was finished the men immediately broke into another.

"Hello?" Granny Relda called out, but the men didn't seem to notice her. They kept up with their violent games, laughing at the top of their lungs. They seemed to be having a lot of fun, despite the fact that two of the men were standing on top of a desk, swords in hand, slashing at one another. Each was an expert swordsman, and not a single blow found its mark. What was strangest about the two men was that each was laughing and complimenting the other on their deadly assaults.

"I should get you out of here," the family's bodyguard squeaked. "These men are barbarians."

"We'll be fine," Granny assured the creature. "I'm told that this is how they behave all the time. We're perfectly safe."

Just then, a potted fern flew past them and smashed against a wall. There was a loud cheer that suddenly died when the men noticed how close they had come to harming the family.

"Gentlemen! We have clients," a huge man with a dark, untamed beard shouted. He must have been more than six-and-a-half-feet tall with a chest as wide as a car bumper and hands as big as basketballs. His eyes were deep-set and fierce, giving him a wild expression that was offset by his wide, beaming smile. "Welcome to the Sherwood Group!"

"Welcome!" the men shouted in unison as they held up their pints of beer.

"I have an appointment with Robin Hood," Granny said.

"Robin Hood!" the girls cried. Sabrina glanced at her sister, waiting for the little girl to squeal with happiness, but Daphne caught her looking.

"No big deal, huh?" Sabrina asked.

Daphne shook her head, though it was obvious she was struggling to hold in her excitement.

One of the sword-fighting men leaped from the desk, thrust his sword in a sheath, and rushed to take Granny's hand. He was a tall, handsome man wearing a dark green pin-striped suit and sporting a red goatee and moustache. His wavy hair hung to his shoulders, framing a broad smile and bushy eyebrows that gave him a mischievous appearance. He looked like the men Sabrina had seen on the covers of romance novels.

He kissed Granny on the hand. "Welcome. I'm Robin Hood, and these miserable louts are my merry men. We're the Sherwood Group, and we've been suing the rich and giving to the poor since 1987."

2

obin Hood and his burly companion led the family down a hallway and into an office lined with floor-to-ceiling windows offering an amazing panorama of the Hudson River. The sun was creeping over the mountains and its rays painted the waves a glittery gold. A tiny sailboat drifted by and a few hungry seagulls hovered over the water searching for breakfast.

Robin Hood's office was tastefully decorated with framed law degrees and shelves of thick legal books. The only things that seemed out of place were a bow strung with a heavy cord, hanging from a shelf above the door, and a quiver of arrows leaning in the corner.

"Mrs. Grimm, please come in," the man said, helping the family into the leather chairs in front of a huge oak desk. The pig-snouted creature scouted the room, peeking into a potted plant and beneath a leather sofa, before it crossed its arms and stationed itself by the door.

"I apologize for the commotion when you came in," Robin said. "You can take the men out of the forest but you can't take the forest out of the men. Allow me to introduce my associate, Little John."

"Happy to meet you," the man roared. Sabrina reached out to shake his hand but he swatted her on the back in what he must have thought was a friendly pat. It nearly knocked Sabrina out of her chair.

"Mr. Hood, these are my granddaughters, Sabrina and Daphne."

"Please call me Robin," he said as he bent over and kissed each girl on the hand. Sabrina nearly fainted. He was so handsome and kind. Her hands got sweaty and her heart started to race. She realized she was staring at him, and worse, she couldn't seem to stop.

"I've heard quite a bit about the famous sisters Grimm," he continued, patting Sabrina on the head like she was a beagle, then turning to shake Granny's hand. "How can I help you, Mrs. Grimm?"

"Robin, I need a lawyer," Granny Relda said.

"Then you've come to the right place. My staff and I are all first-rate lawyers, though admittedly we got our degrees online. I hope that won't be a problem. Ferryport Landing doesn't have a law school, or a college, or even a high school, really." Robin took a seat and put his feet up on the desk, revealing the leather boots he wore instead of loafers. "So, were you injured on the job? A victim of malpractice? Bought some toys with too much lead paint?"

"Actually, I have a friend who has been arrested," Granny said.

Robin and Little John shared a worried look. "The Wolf," Robin said unsteadily as he sat up straight in his chair.

"We prefer to call him Mr. Canis," the old woman replied. "He was arrested a month ago and there are still no charges filed against him. The sheriff is also preventing us from visiting him."

Little John stepped forward. "That's unfortunate, Mrs. Grimm, but I'm not sure we can help. We're not criminal defense lawyers."

"He's right. We're litigators," Robin added. "We sue companies that spill chemicals into rivers or make products that break, and we help people get settlements when they slip on the sidewalk. We've never argued a case in criminal court."

"You must have some training," Granny said. "The only two

criminal defense lawyers who lived in Ferryport Landing were human, and as you know the mayor has run most of us out of town. We're desperate."

Robin Hood got up from his desk and gazed out the window at the river. Little John joined him and the two men talked in low voices for several moments. They seemed to be having an argument, but eventually the men nodded and shook hands. When they were finished, Robin and Little John turned back to the family.

"It would be impossible to reason with Nottingham," Robin said. "He hates me even more than he hates you and your family."

"Hiring us will make your problems a million times worse," Little John replied.

Sabrina looked over at her grandmother. The old woman's hopeful expression began to fade.

"Plus, if I help you, Mayor Heart will shut this office down by sunset," Robin said.

Granny sighed with defeat and stood up. Sabrina and Daphne did the same. "I understand. We won't waste any more of your time."

Suddenly, Robin Hood leaped in front of them. "I didn't say we wouldn't do it!"

"You'll take the case?" the old woman cried.

"We wouldn't pass this up for the world," Little John bellowed.

"It's been a long time since I've been a thorn in Nottingham's side," Robin added with relish.

"I'll get Friar Tuck started on the paperwork," said Little John.

"Good thinking, my large friend." Robin turned to the family. "As for us, we have an appointment with my favorite sheriff!"

• • •

Fifteen minutes later, Sabrina, Daphne, Granny Relda, Robin Hood, and Little John were pushing open the doors of the police station. The ugly little bodyguard, who Sabrina had learned was a miniature orc named Barto, followed behind, darting into alleyways, blocking traffic, and rushing about, fully prepared to leap into combat to protect the group. Sabrina found him painfully annoying but Granny refused to send him home.

The police station was a mess. Boxes of files were scattered about. Many had been tipped over, rummaged through, and abandoned. There were big maps of the town on the walls, some covered in scribbled writing, and the front desk was stained with coffee-cup rings and cigarette burns.

Robin approached the counter and rang a tarnished brass

bell. The chime was answered by an enraged growl from a back room.

"WHAT NOW?" a voice shouted.

"There he is," Robin said as his face broke into a mischievous smile.

"As pleasant as ever," Little John added.

A door flew open, rattling the full-length mirror on the wall behind it. Nottingham barreled into the room like an angry bull. When he spotted the Grimms he snarled, but when he saw Robin and Little John, he reared back on his heels in shock. He examined the group the way a hyena eyes its prey. Sabrina had seen this expression before. He'd had it the night he tried to kill Daphne. It made the purple scar that started at the tip of Nottingham's eye and ended at the corner of his mouth seem to pulsate.

"You!" Nottingham roared as he pointed an angry finger at the lawyers.

"Us," Robin replied. It was obvious to Sabrina that the sheriff and Robin Hood had shared a long, bumpy history and that their friend in the green suit had gotten the better of it. She made a mental note to read up on Robin Hood's adventures when she got a chance.

"Interesting outfit you've got there, Nottingham," Robin continued.

The sheriff was wearing leather pants, and boots that reached his knees. His shirt was black and billowy, with silver buttons carved in the shape of human skulls. He had a long, swishy cape tied at his neck and a sheathed dagger strapped to his waist.

"Is this what they mean when they call something old school?" Little John continued. "You do realize this isn't the fifteenth century?"

"There's nothing old-fashioned about this," Nottingham said, brandishing his dagger.

"Oh, Nottingham, you do enjoy the drama," Robin said. "We didn't come here to fight you. We came to see our client."

"Client? What client?"

"Mr. Canis."

Suddenly, Sheriff Nottingham's rage disappeared and he roared with laughter. "So the mongrel has a lawyer now? Hilarious!"

"I'm glad you're amused," Robin said. "I find what is passing as the rule of law in this town just as funny. You arrested Canis four weeks ago and have yet to charge him with a crime. If you aren't going to charge him you must set him free—that's the law in Ferryport Landing."

"I AM THE LAW!" Nottingham shouted. "I'll do what I want with that monster. He's a murderer and he'll hang if I have anything to say about it."

"I remember a time when you used to say the same thing about me," Robin replied. "As for Canis—a murderer? Who was the victim?"

Nottingham chuckled. "Don't tell me you haven't heard the story? It goes a little something like this: A child wearing a red hood journeyed to visit her poor, sick grandmother. A monster came along and ate the grandmother. No one lived happily ever after."

"That happened six hundred years ago!" Granny exclaimed.

"Justice has no time limit," the sheriff replied.

"Well, if justice is what you're after, then there must be a trial. I need to meet with Canis and prepare his defense," Robin said.

"Dear me, perhaps I am ill. I hear you speak but your words are nonsense. You don't give a rabid dog a trial—you put him to sleep before he can hurt anyone else."

"You're going to kill him?" Sabrina cried.

Daphne burst into tears. Sabrina did her best to comfort her sister, but she was too shocked to speak more.

"Oh, here come the waterworks," the sheriff said, his face full of mocking concern. He bent over and took Daphne's chin in his gloved hand. "Don't cry, little one. Save your tears. You'll need them sooner than you think."

Little John grabbed Nottingham's arm and jerked him away

from the little girl. He took the Sheriff's hand in his own and squeezed and squeezed until Sabrina thought she heard bones snap. Nottingham yanked his hand away.

"Never let it be said that I don't have a kind heart," he growled, caressing his mangled hand. "I'll let you all see your precious pet one last time before he goes off to doggie heaven."

He led the group down a long hallway. Puddles had collected on the floor and a dark green mold was creeping up the walls. At the end of the hallway was an iron door with an enormous lock. Nottingham inserted a key and pushed the heavy door open, and a creak echoed off the walls. Inside, the large room was split into four separate jail cells, two on either side of a walkway down the center. A lone fluorescent light hanging from the ceiling blinked on and off, fighting a losing battle with the room's hungry shadows.

"You've got visitors, mutt," Nottingham said, running his curved dagger along the bars of one of the cells. The high-pitched screech it made pierced Sabrina's eardrums. "Have your talk and make it quick."

Sabrina peered into the darkness. In the far corner a hulking figure huddled against the wall. His limbs were bound to enormous chains. Sabrina felt a familiar tingle, one she felt only in the presence of magic, and guessed the chains were enchanted.

A normal chain could never hold a creature with the strength of the Big Bad Wolf.

As she stepped closer, an odor drifted into her nose: a combination of filth, sweat, and something less identifiable, something wild. It reminded Sabrina of the time her mother had taken the girls to the Bronx Zoo. While they watched the lions in their pit, a zookeeper tossed in slabs of raw meat for the animals. The lions fought over the scraps, roaring and threatening with their heavy claws. A smell rose up from the pit that afternoon that frightened Sabrina. It was the smell of something savage.

Granny approached the cell, seemingly unfazed. She pressed her hands against the bars and stared into the shadows. "Old friend," she said softly.

There was a rustling in the dark and then a deep voice broke the silence.

"Go away, Relda." The voice was tired and rough.

"We've come to help you," Daphne said as she joined her grandmother at the bars. "We hired lawyers. We're going to get you out of here."

Nottingham laughed. He sounded like a hungry rat excited over a piece of cheese.

Robin and Little John joined Granny and Daphne at the bars. Robin took a small recording device out of his suit pocket and turned it on. "Mr. Canis, I'm Robin Hood of the Sherwood Group and this is my partner, Little John. Our firm is working to release you. I'm sure we can clear this up soon. In the meantime, you've been arrested for murder, and it would be in your best interest to tell me everything you remember about the crime."

"You're wasting your time," Canis said. "I have no memory of the event. I rarely know what the Wolf does. I only know it was something horrible."

"You don't remember anything about it? Then how do you know you did it?" Robin asked.

Canis shook his head. "I just do."

Robin and Little John shared a worried look. Sabrina couldn't believe she heard surrender in the old man's voice.

Robin shook his head. "Mr. Canis, I don't think you understand, we—"

Canis leapt to his feet and let out a horrible roar. It was only then that Sabrina realized how much the old man had changed. When he rose to his full height, he was nearly eight feet tall and thickly muscled. His arms were long, and his ugly, taloned hands dragged on the ground. His ears, pointy and sprouting hair, had migrated to the top of his head. His nose was a slippery snout with glistening fangs hanging below, and his shock of white hair was now brown flecked with black. Sabrina's mind reeled. This couldn't be Mr. Canis. How could he have changed so much in four weeks? She was sure this had to be a twisted joke, some kind of terrible prank cooked up by Nottingham for his own amusement. But then she saw the undeniable proof that this creature was her old friend. The beast was wearing a black eye patch on his left eye. It covered a wound that Nottingham had inflicted not long ago. She knew the truth. Canis was losing his battle with the vicious Wolf inside him. Out of instinct, she leaped forward and pulled her sister and grandmother to safety.

"Sabrina!" Granny cried, bewildered. There was disappointment and anger in her voice. "You have nothing to fear from Mr. Canis."

"Do not scold her, Relda," Mr. Canis said. "She might be the only one in your family who sees me for what I am. You'd be wise to pay more attention to her."

Granny shook her head, denying his words.

"What have you done to him?" Daphne demanded, racing at the sheriff with fists clenched. It took all of Sabrina's strength to hold her back.

"Get control over your brats, Mrs. Grimm, or they'll be enjoying the cell next to your friend," Nottingham said.

"Girls, attacking the sheriff won't help Mr. Canis," Granny said, pulling Sabrina and Daphne to her side.

"Nothing can help me," Canis grunted. "Relda, take the girls and leave. I don't need your lawyers or your help. I'm right where I should be. A cage is where I belong."

"Old friend—"

Canis shook his head. "Your old friend is gone."

"That can't be true."

"Not yet . . . but soon," Canis said wearily. "Fighting the Wolf's control over this body is a constant battle, one I am losing. When the war is over, it is best if I am under lock and key."

"That's not going to happen," Daphne said as she pulled away from Granny and approached the cell. She reached through the bars and took Canis's hand in her own, caressing it gently. His was big and strong with nails like railroad spikes. A memory flashed in Sabrina's brain—once, not so long ago, the Wolf had been unleashed and had snatched Sabrina around the neck. He had promised to eat her. The memory made Sabrina shiver down to her toes.

Sheriff Nottingham ran his dagger against the cell bars again. "Time's up!" he shouted. "Get out of my jail."

Little John turned to Mr. Canis. "Don't worry. We'll be back."

Canis crawled back into the shadows, into the corner of his

cell. "Do not waste your time on me, Relda," he whispered as they left.

• • •

That afternoon Robin Hood called to update Granny Relda. As he had predicted, Mayor Heart and Sheriff Nottingham came to the offices of the Sherwood Group with an order to seize the property and premises of the business. The merry partners were tossed out into the street. Robin and Little John were forced to continue their work from an empty table at Sacred Grounds, a coffee shop run by Uncle Jake's girlfriend, Briar Rose. Much to everyone's surprise, Robin and Little John were thrilled.

"He said he and Little John have never been happier," Granny Relda explained when she hung up the phone. "They're Nottingham's biggest annoyance again. I don't know if Briar's coffee shop sells beer but they both sounded rip-roaring drunk."

"Being merry as often as those guys are can't be good for their livers," Uncle Jake said.

Unfortunately, Robin's newfound joy came with some very bad news. He and Little John were running into one roadblock after another. The Ferryport Landing justice system had collapsed since the days when Mayor Charming ran the town. Since Nottingham had become the sheriff, there had been few arrests other than Mr. Canis's. Not a single official document had been filed regarding any crime, and it seemed as if the sheriff and the mayor were making up laws as they went along. No one ever got a trial, so there were no judges to ensure justice.

Worse still, there was nothing the family could do to help. When Granny offered, Robin informed her that the best thing they could do was to stay by the phone and wait for the lawyers to call with an update. So everyone tried to find ways to keep themselves busy. Uncle Jake searched the magic mirror for Goldilocks. Granny busied herself making earthworm crepes. Puck lay on the couch trying to break his personal record for most farts in an hour. Sabrina and Daphne turned their attention to the family's enormous book collection to research everything they could find on the Big Bad Wolf.

Sabrina and Daphne's father had kept fairy-tale stories out of their house, leaving the girls with a tremendous disadvantage now that their jobs were to investigate crimes in the Everafter community. Still, even Sabrina had heard the Wolf's most famous story—Little Red Riding Hood. The way she recalled it, a really lousy mother sent her kid into the woods with a basket of food and everyone was supposed to be surprised when an animal attacked her. Sabrina was wondering what kind of lame parents Red Riding Hood must have had when she noticed the pale and nervous expression on Daphne's face.

"No one told me this story," Daphne said, pointing to the book she was reading.

"What story, *liebling?*" Granny Relda asked as she came in from the kitchen.

Daphne held up a dusty copy of *Children's and Household Tales*, better known as Grimm's Fairy Tales. "The story of Little Red Riding Hood," she said. "Jacob and Wilhelm Grimm called it the story of Little Red Cap. This version is . . . gross."

Granny shook her head knowingly. "It is troubling, but don't forget, Mr. Canis isn't like the Wolf in that story."

Puck, who had been ignoring everyone up until that point, leaped up and rushed across the room. "What did he do?"

"He ate Red's grandmother," Daphne said.

"Ate her?" Sabrina cried.

"That's awesome!" Puck exclaimed.

Sabrina ignored Puck. "I thought he killed her."

"The killing part usually happens when you eat someone," Puck said matter-of-factly.

"That was a long time ago," Granny said. "We weren't there. Some of the story could be exaggerated."

Daphne scanned the old book. "It says here that Red's parents sent her into the forest with a basket of food. She was supposed to take it to her sick grandmother but along the way she met the Wolf. He asked her where she was going and she told him."

"Mistake number one," Puck said.

Daphne continued. "The wolf raced ahead, ate her grandmother, then put on her clothes."

"Creepy," Puck commented.

"Then it says here that when Red showed up at the house he ate her, too. That's not right. Little Red Riding Hood is alive."

"And crazy as ever," Sabrina said. Just thinking about the little girl gave her goose pimples. She calmed down when she remembered Red was locked up in the Ferryport Landing Memorial Hospital's mental health ward. It had been only a few months since the delirious Red had stormed through town on the back of a Jabberwocky, causing serious mayhem.

"You can't put a lot of weight in this story," Granny explained. "There are a lot of contradictory facts that don't add up, and there are many, many versions."

"That's true. Now I remember this story. My father told me it once," Puck said. "Something about a woodcutter who saved Red and her granny by cutting the Wolf's belly open and freeing them. Then I think he loaded the Wolf's belly up with stones and tossed him in the river to drown. I'd like to meet that guy. He's totally hard-core!"

"Who cares how many versions there are of the story? He eats people in all of them, right?" Sabrina asked as she glanced at the open pages of the heavy book. There was a horrible illustration of the Wolf attacking the little girl.

Puck nodded. "Don't forget he tried to kill the Three Little Pigs and a whole family of talking lambs. I tell you, the guy's got anger-management issues."

Sabrina's mind was drowning in all the new information. She turned to her grandmother, who seemed nervous and fidgety. "Did he really do this?"

The room was silent. Granny lowered her eyes.

Sabrina was dumbfounded. "And you let him live here with us? You left us alone with him! He slept in a room right across the hall!"

"The Wolf is the murderer, Sabrina. Mr. Canis is not responsible," Granny said.

"Mr. Canis *is* the Wolf!" Sabrina cried.

"No, you are wrong, Sabrina," Granny snapped. "Mr. Canis and the Wolf are two separate people."

"Who share the same body," Sabrina argued. "Mr. Canis taps into him when he needs his power. He's been changing into the Wolf for months."

"OK, everyone, let's calm down," Daphne said.

But Granny was agitated and kept arguing. "Mr. Canis has always been in charge, or at least he has been since the pigs got ahold of him. It wasn't until recently that he lost control of the creature inside him."

"Granny, you saw him today," Sabrina said. "If we manage to get him out of jail, then what happens? What are we going to do if the Wolf takes over? There will be no way to stop him."

"Sabrina! Mr. Canis is our friend!" the old woman cried.

"Our friend is a bloodthirsty monster!"

Granny's face turned red and her lips quivered in anger. Sabrina had never seen the old woman lose her temper so quickly. Sure, Granny had been angry in the past, but this was something far beyond that.

"Sabrina Grimm, go to your room!"

Sabrina reeled back. "What? I haven't been sent to my room since I was seven years old!"

"Then it's long overdue!"

Sabrina looked around at her family, hoping someone could explain what had happened, but they all had the same expression on their faces. They were angry with her, too. All she did was point out the obvious. Mr. Canis was turning into a vicious killer, and no one knew how to stop it. Wasn't it best for everyone if he was locked up safe and sound?

Outnumbered and bewildered, Sabrina marched up the steps and into her room, slamming the door shut behind her. She threw herself on her bed and fought back tears. Crying would be like admitting to everyone that she was still a child, and worse, that her opinions were no more valid than a little kid's. They could send her to her room but that didn't make her wrong. Someone needed to ask if they weren't all better off with Mr. Canis in a cage.

"Are you well?" a voice asked from beneath the bed.

Sabrina leaped up and backed against the wall. "Who's there?"

"I'm part of your security detail," the voice said. "I'm guarding your bed."

Sabrina groaned. "I could really use some privacy right now."

"Sorry, boss's orders. I can't—"

"If you don't get out from under my bed right now, I'm going to drag you out and punt you through the window."

Sabrina heard scuffling, and a moment later a little creature with a bright-red nose, batlike ears, and furry feet crawled out from under the bed. He brushed himself off and examined Sabrina. "I suppose I could take a coffee break."

Sabrina said nothing, only pointed at the door, and a second later the creature was gone.

She expected her grandmother to come to her, apologize for losing her temper, and tell her that everything was going to be OK. But after several hours, the old woman had still not appeared. Daphne and Uncle Jake were no-shows as well, and so was Puck, whom she would have bet money would come by just to gloat. Elvis poked his head in once. She called to him, but the big dog shook her off and disappeared down the hallway. Even the family pet was against her.

She was hardly surprised. She usually found herself butting heads with the others. Sabrina never seemed to do or say anything right, and she often felt as if she were a constant source of disappointment. It wasn't fair. She had been trying very hard to embrace her responsibilities and had taken up detective training with all her energy. She had discovered she was even good at some of it. She excelled in tracking, clue finding, and self-defense. Just last week Granny had praised Sabrina for her problem-solving skills. Well, how could Sabrina be so smart last week and now be completely wrong about Canis? He himself had told Granny that Sabrina was the only one in the family who saw him for what he was. He had warned them all, and now she was being punished for listening.

Around suppertime, she heard a knock on the door. Someone had left a tray with baked chicken in a gravy that smelled like pureed crayons and blueberries. She took it into her room and picked at it listlessly. After a few bites she pushed it away.

Later that evening there was another knock on the door. It opened slowly and Daphne poked her head inside. "Is it safe to come in yet? The bed troll said you threatened to kick him out a window."

"It's safe. In fact, I'm glad you're here. We need to talk."

"If it's about Mr. Canis, I don't want to hear it. He's our friend."

Daphne entered the room. She sat at the desk, opened a drawer, and took out a little bag. Inside was a string of pearls. She tried them on while Sabrina talked.

"Our friend has a history of eating grandmothers and little girls," Sabrina said. "You don't want that to happen again, do you?"

Daphne shook her head. "He's not like that anymore. You know it, too. We've been here almost eight months and he's never hurt any of us."

"He's changing, Daphne."

"What should we do, then? Leave him in jail? Let Nottingham and Heart kill him? He needs us to rescue him. We are Grimms. This is what we do."

"Well, Grimms are prepared, right? That's what Granny says all the time. We should get the weapon."

Daphne reached into her shirt and pulled out a chain. Hanging on it was a small silver key with safe-deposit box numbers carved into its side. "Mr. Hamstead gave us this for emergencies only."

"This is an emergency," Sabrina urged. "I want Mr. Canis to be safe and sound just like you, but let's face it, the guy is getting hairier and angrier by the day. You saw him freak out at the jail today. What are we going to do if we find a way to free him and he loses control to the Wolf? It's best if we have the weapon, just in case. If Mr. Canis finds a way to fix himself then great—we'll just put it back in the safe-deposit box. Or even better, we could use it to scare off the Scarlet Hand. If whatever is in the box can put the hurt on the Wolf then it can certainly take care of them. We might even be able to get rid of Puck's stupid security team."

"That would be nice. I found an elf in one of my dresser drawers, munching on my socks," Daphne said with a small smile.

"It's best if we're ready for whatever happens. Give me the key. I'll sneak out tonight and go get it."

Daphne was about to take off the necklace when she hesitated. "No. Whatever is in that box is magic, and you shouldn't be around magic at all. You know you're addicted to it. Besides, Mr. Hamstead gave the key to me, so I'm going to decide when we use it."

Sabrina was furious. "Daphne, if this is part of your 'I'm a big girl now' routine you need to cut it out. This is important!"

"I said 'no' and I mean 'no,'" Daphne snapped.

Sabrina was tempted to snatch the necklace right off Daphne's neck, but a knock at the door disracted her. The door creaked open and Uncle Jake entered.

"How's it going?" he asked.

"Great!" Sabrina said. "The whole family hates me. I'm having a fantastic day."

Uncle Jake laughed. "Trust me, you aren't the first person to make my mom angry, especially when it comes to Mr. Canis."

Daphne sat down on the bed. "You've argued with Granny about him, too?"

"Sure. So did your grandfather *and* your father," Uncle Jake replied. He sat down at their father's desk and ran his hand over the wooden top. "When Canis first came to live with us, it was all of us against Mom. We all felt like you do now, Sabrina."

"I don't hate him," Sabrina said. "I'm just pointing out that he's changing. Why is she getting angry when I tell the truth?"

"Because after all this time you still fail to give Canis the benefit of the doubt, and Sabrina, he deserves it. When he showed up on our doorstep, my father refused to help him, but Mom has always seen the good in people. She invited him to live here and it drove my dad nuts. He was sure Canis would change back and eat us all in the dead of night. Your father and I used to block our bedroom door with heavy furniture when we went to bed. We used to sleep with baseball bats under our pillows. We were terrified of him."

"If all of you felt like that, then how come I'm the bad guy now?" Sabrina said.

"'Cause we were wrong back then and you are wrong now. Canis has proven over and over that he can be trusted. He's saved all of our lives a million times over, and he has never allowed anyone to lay a hand on my mom. He has been the best friend she ever had and a good friend to me. When the Jabberwocky killed my father, Canis went and dug the grave. I was destroyed by what happened. I blamed myself and didn't even stick around for his funeral. I decided to leave." Jake leaned back in his chair, remembering. "I found Canis waiting for me on the edge of town, and he begged me to stay. He told me my family needed me, but I wouldn't listen. He told me he knew I'd come back and he would watch over my family for me until I returned. Then he gave me a hug."

"No way!" Daphne cried.

"It was the most uncomfortable hug of my life, but I knew I was leaving my family in good hands. I've never spoken badly about Canis since, and I never will again."

"That's fine, but you've seen him. He even told us to leave him alone," Sabrina argued.

"Yes, he's giving up on himself, but my mother never will and that's why she's mad at you, kid. You're giving up on him. She wants you to believe in him like she does and you don't. It breaks her heart. Listen, I didn't come in here to give you a lecture. In fact, the *warden* has given me permission to release you," he said.

"Is Granny still mad?" Daphne asked.

"Let's just say the last time I saw her like this, your father and I had just been arrested for using a magic wand to turn a teacher into a billy goat. Ms. Junger nearly ate her own desk before Mom forced us to change her back . . . Now, your grandmother thinks the two of you can help me."

"With what?" Sabrina asked.

"Tracking down our elusive Goldilocks," he said, gesturing out into the hall.

Suddenly, the argument was forgotten and the girls rushed down the hallway, eager to help their uncle find the mysterious lady. Mirror was waiting for them when they arrived.

"Mirror, show the girls what you just showed me," Uncle Jake said.

"Jake, you know how this works. Poetry activates the magic," Mirror replied.

Daphne stepped up to the reflection. "Mirror, Mirror, my greatest wish is to know where Goldilocks is."

Mirror frowned.

"What?" Daphne said. "It rhymes!"

"Hardly! *Is* and *wish* do not rhyme."

"It's close enough!"

"Where is the rhythm? And the grammar—atrocious!"

"Listen, if you want poetry, read some Maya Angelou," Uncle Jake said. "Just show us Goldilocks."

Mirror frowned but did as he was asked. Goldilocks appeared in the silver surface. She was standing on the second-floor balcony of an elegant hotel. Behind her, through a glass doorway, Sabrina could see a king-size poster bed and an expensive-looking antique dresser. There were vines climbing up to the balcony and pretty boats floating along the sun-dappled water below. Goldilocks looked radiant as the sunshine lit up her face.

"She sure is pretty," Daphne said.

Uncle Jake smiled. "Your dad always had great taste in women, though I never understood what they saw in him."

Sabrina glanced over to her sleeping father. From what she had managed to piece together, Goldilocks and Henry had had a relationship before he met Sabrina's mother. She had been told they were deeply in love but the tragedy that killed Grandpa

Basil had split them apart. With the help of Uncle Jake, Goldilocks was freed from Ferryport Landing, the first Everafter to leave in two hundred years. Henry left soon after to start a new life in New York City, free of Everafters. That's where he met the girls' mother.

Goldilocks was not at all how Sabrina had imagined her. She had somehow assumed the mysterious Everafter would resemble her own mother, Veronica, but they were complete opposites. Goldilocks seemed young—almost immature—and there was a look of wonder and curiosity in her eyes. She was always wearing dresses and her hair was never out of place. Sabrina's mom was an ebony-haired woman who could have easily been a beauty queen in her own right, but she had an easy, casual way about her. She loved blue jeans and flip-flops, baseball caps and sunshine. Sabrina realized she was comparing the two women, and a twinge of betrayal sent a jolt of pain into her heart. Her father might have loved this strange Everafter once, and Goldilocks might be pretty, but she was no Veronica Grimm. Sabrina thought her mother was the best thing that ever happened to her dad.

"I've been watching her since yesterday," Uncle Jake said. "After her little trip in the desert, she headed to the airport and hopped on a flight. I couldn't tell which one, but she seemed like she was in a hurry. She didn't even check any bags."

The image in the mirror dissolved, only to be replaced with a view of a flag fluttering from a banister. It was bright red with a border of thorny vines, and on each corner and side there were small figures that looked like saints. In total there were six figures, not including the golden winged lion at its center. The lion wore a shimmering halo and stood guard over a castle on a hill. Sabrina had never seen anything like it and wanted to study it further, but once again, the image changed. This time they saw a mailbox. It was labeled 10 and was stuffed with mail. Sabrina peered at the letters, hoping an address might reveal itself, but what little she could make out was not written in English. Then the mailbox was gone, too, replaced by an elegant sign mounted on the side of a luxury hotel. The sign read HOTEL CIPRIANI.

Uncle Jake was smiling from ear to ear. "Cool, huh?"

"I'm confused," Sabrina said. "We've been watching her travel around for a month. What's different about this time?"

"The difference is we have the name of her hotel!" Uncle Jake exclaimed. "We can write her a letter! Beg her to come back! All we have to do now is find out where this hotel is located. I think that odd flag we saw might be a big clue. If we can find the country it belongs to we can narrow down our search. The language looks like Italian, but that doesn't necessarily mean she's in Italy. Italian is spoken all over the world—she could be in Slovenia, San Marino—Italian is even an official language of Switzerland."

"And how do you suggest we learn all this?" Sabrina asked.

"The library, of course," Uncle Jake said.

Sabrina groaned. "Not the library."

"What's wrong with the library?" Uncle Jake asked.

"Nothing. The library is fine. It's the librarian that's the problem," Sabrina said.

"He's a complete idiot," Daphne explained.

"I thought he was supposed to be the smartest guy in the world," Uncle Jake said.

"Maybe, but he's still an idiot," Sabrina said. "Why can't you go?"

Uncle Jake shook his head. "Someone's got to stay here and keep an eye on Goldilocks."

"We're going to need the flying carpet to get to the library," Sabrina said as she reached into her pants pocket for her set of keys to the Hall of Wonders. But before she could hand them over to Mirror, Puck entered the room.

"Uh-uh-uh-uh-uh," he said. "You two aren't going anywhere without protection."

"Well, you can forget sending one of your misfits with us," Sabrina said. "In fact, you can get rid of the whole team."

"Listen, dogface. Almost everyone in this town wants you dead. Not that I can blame them. But if you were to die, I know the old lady would want to have a funeral, and if there's a funeral I know I'm going to have to take a bath. So I will superglue a hobgoblin to your leg if I have to," Puck declared.

Sabrina was so angry she thought she might burst into flames. It wasn't that Puck was being stubborn about his stupid security team; it was because he called her dogface. She knew it shouldn't have mattered. He insulted her all the time, but for some reason this one stung. Why did it suddenly matter to her that he thought she was ugly?

"What? No comeback?" Puck pressed, clearly surprised.

"Maybe Puck can fly us to the library?" Daphne suggested.

"Excellent idea," Uncle Jake said.

"Boring!" Puck cried.

"Oh, I'm sorry, I was under the impression that you were some kind of mischief maker. I remember a time when you would have jumped at the chance to sneak out without my mother knowing," Uncle Jake said. "Oh, well. I guess you've lost your touch."

Puck scowled. "I have not lost my touch for mischief! I invented mischief!"

"These days you seem to act more like a good little boy than someone called the Trickster King. In fact, I'm surprised that people don't mistake you for that other beloved flying boy that won't grow up. What's his name?"

"Don't you say it!" Puck warned.

"I know who you're talking about," Daphne added, winking at her uncle. "The one that hangs out with the little girl and her brothers. He can fly, too. What's his name?"

"I mean it! Don't you say his name in front of me. That guy is a washed-up has-been. Don't you even compare us!"

"Oh, I remember," Uncle Jake said. "You're acting like Peter—"

Puck let out an angry bellow. "FINE!" he shouted. "I'll go with you but let's get something straight. I am not some goofy flying boy in green tights. I am the Trickster King: the spiritual leader of hooligans, good-for-nothings, pranksters, and class clowns. I am a villain feared worldwide and don't you forget it."

"Of course you are," Uncle Jake said.

Two enormous insectlike wings popped out of Puck's back. They stood taller than his body, and when he flapped them, the wind they created blew Sabrina's hair around. He buzzed right over Sabrina's and Daphne's heads, snatching the girls off their feet and whisking them out the open bedroom window. Sabrina saw her uncle wave good-bye as she soared over the forest, bright with the setting sun's palette of oranges, reds, and yellows.

3

The Mid-Hudson Public Library was a small, squat building not far from the train station. Its parking lot was empty, as was the lot for the tiny auditorium next to it. When humans had lived in the town, the little library had been a bustling community center. Now that they were gone, it was lonely and dark. It reminded Sabrina of the westerns her mother loved to watch on television. They all seemed to be set in the same barren ghost town. The library had the same abandoned feel. She expected tumbleweeds to roll by at any moment.

Puck lowered the girls to the ground outside the library's front door, and his wings tucked themselves back under his hoodie. He sniffed the air and crinkled up his nose.

"I smell books," he said, repulsed.

"That's probably because this is a library," Sabrina said, rolling her eyes. "It's full of books."

"No way! Why didn't you warn me?"

"What did you think a library was?" Daphne asked.

"I don't know," Puck cried. "I was hoping it was a place where men fought tigers with their bare hands. I should have known better. You guys never want to do anything fun."

"Oh, you're not going to be bored in here," Daphne said.

"Yeah, I'm warning you in advance," Sabrina said to the fairy boy. "You need to stay alert in here. The librarian is sort of unpredictable."

"We should have brought the football helmets," Daphne said to her sister.

Sabrina nodded. "You're right. We keep forgetting."

"You two are teasing me," Puck complained.

"Fine! Don't believe us," Sabrina said. "You'll see soon enough."

She led them through the front door. Inside, the library was a disastrous mess. Books, magazines, and newspapers lay scattered about the floor as if a cyclone had blown them off their shelves. Everywhere she looked, Sabrina saw piles of papers and overturned chairs but not a single soul.

Puck's face turned green as if he was about to be sick. "Look at all the learning," he moaned. "I'm going to lose my lunch."

Sabrina grabbed his hand and pulled him down an aisle lined with packed bookshelves. "Let's just find what we're looking for and get out of here. If we're lucky we won't have to see the librarian at all."

Daphne took one side and Sabrina took the other, scanning the titles as they walked and hoping they might stumble upon a book of international flags. They found nothing, so they headed up another aisle. As they searched, Puck gagged.

"Can you give it a rest?" Sabrina asked.

"The smell is horrible! Books reek!" Puck cried. "It's so bad I can almost taste them."

"Stop being a baby," Daphne said. Her tone startled Sabrina. She had never heard the little girl scold anyone, especially Puck. Daphne usually thought everything he said or did was hilarious. Worse still was the expression on her sister's face. Daphne was impatiently rolling her eyes again. It was the rudest thing Sabrina had ever seen her do and it made her furious. She was just about to give her sister a lecture on manners when she heard someone whistling happily from across the room. Sabrina groaned. The librarian had found them.

"Is that the lunatic you were talking about?" Puck said, searching for the owner of the whistle.

Sabrina nodded. "Remember what we told you. Stay on your toes."

"Hello!" the librarian cried as he appeared from around a

shelf. He was holding a towering stack of books that reached several feet over his head. "It's the Grimm sisters. You know, since the last time you were here, I was thinking how clever and funny your name is—the Sisters Grimm—oh, that's fun. Like the Brothers Grimm—only girls."

"Yes, it's hilarious," Sabrina said, forcing a smile on her face. "Do you need any help?"

"Everything is under control," the librarian said, but his words did not reflect reality. With each step, the tower of books swayed back and forth. Convinced that the stack would topple over and crush them at any moment, Sabrina shuffled the group to the left, then to the right. It seemed as if no matter what direction they moved, the swaying books followed.

"I suppose you are hot on the trail of another mystery," the librarian continued, unaware of the impending disaster.

"Are you sure you don't need a hand?" Daphne asked.

"I'm hunky-dory!" the librarian claimed, but he was wrong. The top book in his stack slipped off. The librarian's right leg darted out and the book landed on his foot before it hit the ground. He stood balanced on one leg, yet perfectly content. With one foot holding the book, the odd gentleman was forced to hop up and down on his free leg toward the information desk. Unfortunately, his hopping made the tower drift even farther, keeping Sabrina, Daphne, and Puck on the move to avoid the avalanche.

Just as the librarian reached the desk, a banana peel slipped out of his pocket.

"OH! I'm losing my lunch!" he cried.

Sabrina sighed, knowing full well what was about to happen. She'd seen the same thing the last time they had visited the librarian, except then it had been an orange peel. She watched helplessly as he stepped on the banana peel and went flailing forward, showering the children with heavy books and knocking them to the ground. Sabrina caught one right between the eyes and saw little stars explode in front of her face.

Puck managed to snatch his sword and bat the books away, then he brushed himself off frantically as if the books had been poisonous spiders. "Get them off me!" he shouted.

"Oh, my! Clumsy me," the librarian cried as he struggled to his feet. He tried to help the children up but stepped on the banana peel again and lost his footing once more. This time he did a complete somersault in midair and landed flat on his back. When he got to his feet, Sabrina could see his true Everafter form. Hay sprang from the collar and sleeves of his red plaid shirt. A dusty old hat sat on his head, and his kindly face was nothing more than an old burlap sack with eyes, nose, and mouth crudely painted on it. He was the Scarecrow, made famous in L. Frank Baum's Oz books. Watching the face, with its moving mouth and blinking eyes, was too much for Sabrina's sensitive stomach, and like Puck, she suddenly felt nauseated. She had to avert her eyes when Scarecrow talked, just to keep her lunch in her belly. She knew it was rude, but not as rude as barfing all over the card catalog. She wondered if she'd ever get used to seeing such strange things.

Puck leaped into the air. His wings kept him high above the piles of books. He darted around the librarian like an annoying gnat.

"You're a scarecrow," he said.

"Actually, I'm *the* Scarecrow, accomplished thinker, former Emperor of Oz, and head librarian of the Mid-Hudson Public Library."

Puck eyed the man closely. "But you're made out of hay, right?"

"Yes, and a brain. The great and terrible Oz gave it to me before he flew away in his balloon."

"Someone gave you a brain?" Puck asked. "I'm actually jealous. Whose was it before you got it?"

"I'm not sure what you mean," Scarecrow stammered.

"The brain! Oz had to have gotten it somewhere. I bet it was a deranged killer's. Those are the easiest to get."

The Scarecrow stifled a scream. "My brain was brand new!"

"As if!" Puck said. "I know Oz and he never bought anything that wasn't on sale. I'm sure your brain is secondhand."

The Scarecrow looked as if he might have a nervous breakdown, so Sabrina stepped in to change the subject. "We're looking for a friend who is overseas. We have a street address and a flag but not a city or a country."

"Well, you came to the right place," the librarian exclaimed as he got himself under control. "Tell me about this flag of yours."

"It's red with a big golden lion in the center," Daphne said. "The lion has wings and is guarding a castle on a hill. There're all these vines on the border and little saints in the corners, too."

Scarecrow rubbed his burlap chin, thought for a moment, and then his eyes lit up. "I've seen that flag!" He raced off, leaving the children behind. They chased the Scarecrow through the stacks and caught up with him in the back of the library. He was already climbing up a big bookcase, reaching for a book on the very top. The bookcase was not mounted to the wall and was teetering back and forth under the Scarecrow's weight.

"Does anyone else see where this is going?" Sabrina sighed. She remembered seeing the movie *The Wizard of Oz* when she was a child. The Scarecrow was such a klutz, Sabrina would giggle whenever he was on-screen. The real flesh-and-hay Scarecrow wasn't much different, but the pratfalls weren't as endearing. Perhaps she was getting older and had less patience for such silliness, or maybe, she suspected, the Scarecrow was just annoying. "I think I know why Dorothy wanted to go back to Kansas," Sabrina muttered to herself.

Despite the Scarecrow's weight, the shelf did not topple over, but that didn't mean Sabrina and Daphne were safe. The Scarecrow kept tossing down the books he didn't need. The tumbling volumes were encyclopedias, and the children darted around like they were trapped in a whack-a-mole game.

"Here it is," the Scarecrow cried, just before he fell off the shelf and landed in a heap on the floor. Without missing a beat, the librarian sprang to his feet and opened the book. Inside were pictures of flags from all over the world. He flipped through the pages until he found a flag that looked just like the one the girls had seen hanging from the Hotel Cipriani's banister. "Is that it?"

Daphne and Sabrina nodded.

"That's the flag of a city called Venice," the Scarecrow said, quite proud of his discovery. "It's a lovely place built on one hundred seventeen islands connected by one hundred fifty canals. In Venice, you don't hail a cab, you hail a boat called a gondola, because many of the roads are actually waterways. The

population is roughly two hundred and fifty thousand people. The average annual rainfall is thirty-four inches. The major industry is tourism, and the region's biggest exports are textiles, clothing, glass, paper, motor vehicles, chemicals, minerals, and nonferrous metals."

Sabrina prepared for Daphne to ask for the definition of *nonferrous*; she herself had no idea what it meant. But much to Sabrina's surprise, the little girl took a pocket dictionary from her purse and looked up the word on her own.

"*Nonferrous* is a metal containing little or no iron," she announced.

Sabrina grabbed the dictionary. "What's this?"

"What does it look like?" Daphne said, rolling her eyes.

Sabrina could feel her face tighten up. How dare Daphne roll her eyes at her!

"Now, how about that hotel?" the Scarecrow asked, interrupting the argument.

"It's called Hotel Cipriani," Daphne said, since Sabrina was still too angry to talk.

"Sounds like that language they speak over there," Scarecrow said. "What's it called? You know, the language they speak in Italy?"

"Uh . . . Italian?" Daphne asked.

"Bingo!" Scarecrow raced back through the library to where travel books for places all around the world were kept. Soon the girls were caught in another hailstorm of books. Copies of *Fodor's Guide to Oz*, *Frommer's Lilliput*, *Lonely Planet's Narnia*, and *The Complete Idiot's Guide to Neverland* flew at them. After some very close calls, Scarecrow snatched a book off a shelf and held it triumphantly above his head. "Here it is!" In his excitement, he lost his balance and nearly fell off the bookcase. He managed to hold on with one hand, but he struggled to regain his footing.

"Oh, yeah, that's a secondhand brain, for sure," Puck said, flying down to the girls' level. "Oz was such a prankster."

"Have you forgotten that Oz tried to kill us?" Sabrina said.

"You can be a homicidal madman and hilarious at the same time, you know," Puck said—right before the bookcase tipped over and came crashing down, burying him in a mountain of books.

"Boy, am I accident prone today," the librarian said.

"The books! They're touching me," Puck groaned. "They're all over me!"

"We'll get this off you in no time," the Scarecrow said. Working together, he and the girls lifted the heavy shelf off Puck. When he got to his feet, Sabrina noticed he had blotchy red marks on his arms and legs, and his face had swollen to the size of a pumpkin.

"I'm allergic!" he cried as he scratched his arms and legs furiously. He reached for the wooden sword he kept at his waist. Sabrina was sure Puck was going to attack the clumsy scarecrow, but instead, he used his weapon to scratch the areas of his back that he couldn't reach. "Whoever had your brain before you was evil!" Puck muttered.

Scarecrow frowned, but then he spotted a book on the floor and his burlap face lit up. "Hey! Here's the book." He grabbed a large volume off the floor, then opened it and flipped through the pages. "This is a travel guide to Italian hotels. Travel books don't get checked out much. There aren't too many vacationers from Ferryport Landing. Oh, here it is—the Hotel Cipriani. It has a five-star rating—very swanky."

"Is there an address for the hotel?" Sabrina asked, remembering her uncle's specific request.

"Absolutely! The listing says it's at Giudecca 10 in Venice," Scarecrow said. "They put the building number after the street name in a lot of European countries. Is there anything else you need to know?"

"I'm not sure we'd survive any more of your help," Daphne grumbled. "Thanks a lot."

"No thanks is necessary!" Scarecrow said, ignoring Daphne's comment. "Learning something new is thanks enough. Though I could use a hand reshelving some of these books."

The Scarecrow strolled away, leaving the shelf and the books where they fell. Puck fired insults at him as the librarian walked away. "I know Oz. He's a liar. I wouldn't be surprised if your brain wasn't made out of an old sock and some butterscotch pudding! I'm talking to you, Mr. Genius. You should call Oz and get the receipt for your brain. I'm sure the warranty has expired."

"We tried to warn you," Daphne said as she picked up a travel guide to Camelot and put it back on a shelf.

"*We tried to warn you,*" Puck mocked as he scratched furiously. "Oh, I can smell the books on my skin!"

Though Puck refused, Sabrina and Daphne decided to help the Scarecrow with the mess he made. After an hour they were regretting their decision.

"Books are heavy," Daphne grumbled as she reshelved a series of increasingly thick novels about a boy who went to a school for wizards.

"I know. Can't they write these things smaller?" Sabrina said.

"Excuse me," a voice said from behind them. Sabrina hadn't heard anyone approach and nearly screamed when she turned around. Standing before her was the strangest-looking man she had ever seen. He wore an expensive-looking white suit and his fingers were adorned with silver and ruby rings. On his wrist was a diamond-studded watch and in his ears were small silver hoop earrings. But what really made him stand out was his hair. His long curly beard and bushy eyebrows were an unnatural shade of blue.

"Do you work here?" he asked.

Sabrina shook her head, speechless.

"No, we're just helping out the librarian," Daphne said. The little girl stammered a bit, obviously disturbed by the man as well.

The man with the blue hair frowned and looked about. "That fool will be no help. I don't suppose you can point me to the law books?"

Sabrina shrugged. "Sorry."

"I'll find them myself," the man huffed and walked farther into the library.

Sabrina looked after him. There was something troubling about this stranger. She felt as if there was evil rather than blood pumping through his veins. His hair and glaring eyes seemed inhuman, like he was the devil made flesh.

"Do you know who that was? That's Bluebeard," Puck said as

he pulled the girls behind a shelf. "He's got to be the most villainous Everafter in this town."

"I thought you were the most villainous Everafter in this town," Sabrina said.

"Besides me," Puck said as he peered around the corner. "He's a recluse. I hear he has a mansion up on Mount Taurus, but no one has seen him in years. I heard Charming told him to stay out of town. I guess now that there's a new mayor, he's doing what he wants."

"So what? Who's Bluebeard?" Sabrina asked impatiently.

Puck wrapped his hand around her mouth. "Shhhh!" he whispered, then turned back to watch the man. "Bluebeard is famous for being married almost fifty times, and each of his wives had a nasty habit of losing her head."

"You mean he drove them crazy?" Daphne asked.

"No, I mean he chopped their heads off with an ax, duh!" Puck snapped.

"Gross!" Daphne said, peering around the corner to get a better look at the man.

"That's only half of it," Puck said. "He stored his wives' bodies in a secret room in his home. He used the room to test his new wives. He forbade them from entering it and if curiosity got the best of them, he added them to his collection."

"If he's so evil, why are we standing here watching him?" Sabrina said.

"'Cause I'm trying to get up the courage to go over and ask him for an autograph," Puck said.

Sabrina watched Bluebeard study a shelf holding several leather-bound books. He took a few large volumes off the shelf and put them on a nearby table. When he had a big pile, he sat and started flipping through them and taking notes.

"What do you think he's doing here?" Daphne asked.

No one knew, and it was clear that they shouldn't stick around to find out. The man made Sabrina nervous. Even from across the library she could feel the darkness inside him. It felt hot and angry.

Unfortunately, before they could leave, they were stopped in their tracks by a familiar face. Snow White had several books in her hands and she set them down at an empty table near where Bluebeard was studying. Snow White was stunning, with creamy white skin, coal-black hair, and twinkling blue eyes. Her beauty was so profound it seemed unnatural, as if she didn't belong to the human race.

"Should we say hi?" Daphne whispered.

Snow White had been a good family friend, but none of the Grimms had heard a peep from her in more than a month. She was very angry with Granny Relda, so angry that their friendship was in ruins. Granny had let Snow's former fiancé, Prince Charming, sleep on the family couch when everyone thought he was missing and maybe dead. Snow, heartbroken with fear and worry, felt betrayed when she discovered he was safe and sound and hiding in her best friend's home. Sabrina couldn't blame Ms. White. Charming should have told her where he was, but he claimed Snow's life was in danger. He wanted to save her without her knowing it, but his plan blew up in everyone's face when Snow dropped by unexpectedly and discovered him alive and well.

Unfortunately, the beauty's arrival at the library was noticed by Bluebeard as well. Snow White's presence tore his attention away from his books; he seemed hypnotized by her. He studied her the way an art collector looks at a rare painting. His gaze didn't fall on her so much as it seemed to reach out for her, coaxing her to come closer. Sabrina was reminded of a film she had seen in school about spiders catching flies in their webs then eating them from the inside out.

"Snow White?" Bluebeard said, standing up from his table.

Snow turned to face him, her ever-present smile lighting up the room. When she saw him her grin faded. "Oh, hello, Mr. Bluebeard."

"Snow, I haven't seen you in years. You're looking wonderful," Bluebeard said as his eyes darted over her body.

"Thank you," the teacher muttered. Sabrina could tell Ms. White was nervous. The beauty dropped one of the books she was holding. Bluebeard swooped down and retrieved it, but he didn't hand it back, ignoring Snow's outstretched hand.

"It's such a small town, but I never run into you like this," Bluebeard continued.

"Well, I keep quite busy."

"Oh, it's good to be busy. Keeps the mind from wandering," the man said. "You know what they say, 'idle hands are the devil's playground.'"

Sabrina watched Snow force a smile onto her face and nod.

"We really don't get to see enough of each other," Bluebeard continued. "Perhaps I can persuade you to accompany me to dinner. I'd love to 'catch up,' as they say."

Ms. White squirmed. "I'm afraid I'm very busy."

Bluebeard's eyes flashed with anger. "You're saying 'no' to me?"

Snow stood up, knocking her books to the ground, but Bluebeard shoved her back into her chair.

"I'm trying to be nice, Ms. White," he hissed.

"We have to stop this," Daphne declared.

"What do you want to do?" Sabrina asked.

Daphne was about to march up to them and interrupt when Puck grabbed her by the back of the collar. He murmured, "Listen, this isn't a guy you play around with. If you go over there and get into his business, he'll turn his anger on you."

"She needs our help," Daphne said.

Sabrina glanced around, looking for something that might distract Bluebeard. All she saw were books, and rows and rows of shelves. They couldn't exactly start tossing books at a man who cut people's heads off. Then she spotted the Scarecrow. He was at the top of a bookcase, halfway across the room, and as before, the case was teetering back and forth. Sabrina got an idea.

"Help me push this bookcase over," Sabrina said. She pushed on the frame and it leaned a little. With Daphne and Puck helping it was soon rocking back and forth, but with all the books weighing it down, the bookcase seemed like it might fall back and collapse on them.

"I think we need a little something extra," Sabrina said to Puck. The boy grinned, spun around on his heels, and, in a flash, he morphed into a bull with long, white horns. He huffed and stomped his feet.

"We should get out of his way," Sabrina said, pulling her sister aside. With a bellow and a grunt, Puck ran forward, head first, knocking the bookcase hard. It toppled over, crashing into another bookcase right next to it and causing that one to fall over, too. That bookcase fell onto the bookcase beside it, starting a chain reaction throughout the library like dominoes. Books and magazines flew into the air, as did the Scarecrow, who was buried beneath them.

"Oops," Sabrina said, as she, Puck, and Daphne dashed toward the doors. Snow was right in front of them, hurrying to the parking lot. Once outside, they found Ms. White leaning against her car and breathing hard. She was obviously unnerved by her encounter with Bluebeard and was doing her best to calm herself.

"Are you OK, Ms. White?" Daphne asked.

"Daphne?" Snow replied. "Yes, I just ran into . . . well . . ."

"We know," Sabrina said. "Bluebeard."

"Yes," Snow said. "He's always had a thing for me but I . . . wait a minute, are the three of you responsible for all that chaos?"

Puck nodded and bowed. "At your service."

"Why haven't you returned any of Granny Relda's calls?" Daphne asked. "She wants to apologize."

"Daphne, when you grow up you'll find that being an adult is complicated. It's not as easy as picking up the phone and saying 'hi.'"

"First of all, I am grown up," Daphne said. "Second, you don't understand. Granny feels terrible about what happened. Mr. Charming begged us to keep it a secret. He said he was doing it for your own good."

"How is pretending to be dead supposed to be for my own good?" Snow asked.

Sabrina and Daphne shared a knowing glance. "I wish we could tell you but he's sworn us to secrecy," Sabrina said.

"See, that's the problem," Ms. White said. "Everyone is keeping secrets from me and they tell me that it's for my own good."

"We're trying to protect you," Daphne said.

Snow White groaned. "Everyone wants to protect Snow White. Well, I'm not a little girl, Daphne. I was fighting my own battles before Billy Charming came along."

There was a long, uncomfortable silence until Snow spoke again. "The three of you should get home. Relda is probably worried sick about you."

Then she turned, got into her car, and drove away.

• • •

Uncle Jake was thrilled with the information they had gathered at the library. But when Daphne offered to write the letter to Goldilocks, Jake shook his head. He claimed he had made a call to some old friends and they were sending something that would work a lot better than a stamp and an envelope. In fact, he promised their search would soon be over. When the girls and Puck headed off to bed, Jake was still staring at Goldilocks through the mirror. She was in a boat riding on a canal. A man with a long pole steered her along as she glanced up at the moon.

The next morning Sabrina woke to loud shouting and pounding. She rubbed her eyes and looked around, not surprised to find that Daphne was still sound asleep. She climbed out of bed, slipped on a robe she had hanging from her bedpost, and stomped down the stairs. By the front door, poking his head out of the umbrella stand, she found a creature that looked like it was part dwarf, part crocodile. He gestured to the door.

"There's a man out there," the creature hissed. "He could be dangerous." He held a walkie-talkie to his face and cried, "Where's my backup?"

Sabrina looked through the window and saw Robin Hood pounding on the door.

"That's Robin Hood. We know him," Sabrina explained.

"Cancel that backup, people!" the creature shouted into his walkie-talkie. "We are back to code yellow. All clear. I repeat, we are at code yellow." Then he sunk his head back into the stand and disappeared.

Sabrina quickly straightened her hair, tightened her bathrobe, and checked herself in the hall mirror. She could just die, letting the handsome lawyer see her in her goofy pajamas and with a serious case of bed head, but she seemed to be the only one awake and he kept shouting that there was an emergency. Finally, when she realized nothing would make her look better short of a shower, she opened the door.

"You're not dressed! Kid, you've got to get dressed," the lawyer exclaimed as he barged through the open doorway. "Where is everyone?"

Sabrina was horrified to be called a kid. "In bed. It's not even eight in the morning," she said, awkwardly pushing her hair behind her ear.

"Well wake them up! We have to get over to the courthouse, now," Robin cried. "The trial is starting today!"

"What trial?"

"The trial of the Big Bad Wolf," he said.

4

ittle John sent over a demand for a trial last night," Robin Hood said as he hurried the family up the steps of the Ferryport Landing Municipal Courthouse. "To be honest, after our little run-in with Nottingham yesterday I never guessed they would grant us one. Then my partner, Will Scarlet, was filing a class-action suit and noticed the grand jury's schedule posted on the wall."

"Why wouldn't we be informed of the trial ahead of time?" Granny Relda asked.

"Because Heart and Nottingham are trying to catch us off guard," Little John bellowed as they met him at the top of the stairs. "If they can present their case without a defense then the trial could be over within minutes."

"So they're pulling a fast one," Uncle Jake said.

"Absolutely," Robin replied, "but they've forgotten how fast I can be. We'll put a stop to this."

"Do you have anything prepared?" Granny asked.

The lawyers shook their heads. "No, but there's nothing to worry about," Little John said. "After we ask the judge for a postponement, we'll have plenty of time to prepare."

Sabrina watched Daphne take out her dictionary. "Daphne, *postponement* means that they want more time before the trial begins."

Daphne scowled and put her dictionary away. "I don't need your help."

Robin and Little John hurried the group through the front doors, up a flight of marble stairs, and into the courtroom. Sabrina was startled to find that the room was packed with Everafters. Goblins, witches, fairy godmothers, winkies, munchkinlanders, talking animals, and countless more were all excitedly discussing the trial. There were few empty seats left.

Past the audience gallery, Sabrina noticed the jury box—two rows of seats set apart on the far side of the room. Each row contained six people for a total of twelve, and each juror was more bizarre than the last. The Cheshire Cat was one of them, as was Glinda the (not-so) Good Witch. There was also an enormous snail smoking a hookah pipe, a talking sheep, a young man dressed entirely in blue, and, much to Sabrina's horror, an enormous egg with arms, legs, and a face. The top of its body was cracked but whatever was inside was still intact. Sabrina recognized most of them from around town or from one of the many books the family had on Everafters. Only one was a mystery to her. He wore a black hood that kept his face in shadow.

At the front of the room was a wooden chair on a raised platform. Next to it was a much taller podium where a short, oddly shaped man with a tremendous head was sitting. He had an unruly mane of white hair stuffed under a big black top hat and a nose so incredibly large Sabrina suspected Lilliputians could live in his nostrils. He wore a long, black robe and held a carpenter's hammer in his hand. Sabrina guessed he was the judge.

Watching over the crowd were three card soldiers. Sabrina had run into their kind before. Their limbs and heads were human but their bodies were huge playing cards. They acted as Mayor Heart's personal guards. The Three of Clubs seemed to be guarding the judge, while the Five of Diamonds and the Seven of Spades watched the doorway.

There was heavy pounding on the door and the guards opened it. Several more card soldiers filed in, pulling the heavy chains attached to Mr. Canis. They forced him into a seat behind a big desk, then ran the chains through an iron ring fastened to the floor. Canis looked tired, but he grew angry when he spotted the family.

"What are you doing here?" he growled.

"We came to help, of course," Granny Relda said.

"I don't want your help!"

"Order!" the judge demanded, pounding on his desk with the hammer. Sabrina had seen judges use gavels on TV, but never real hammers. With each pound of the tool, splinters from the desk shot into the air. "Order! What is this commotion in my courtroom?"

Robin Hood and Little John rushed to the judge's bench and bowed respectfully. "Your honor, we apologize to the court for our tardiness. We're counselors for Mr. Canis."

"Do you think you can show up for court whenever you want to, counselors?" the judge roared. "I should have the two of you thrown out of here on your ears."

The outburst caused quite a bit of excited chatter, which enraged the judge even further. He slammed his hammer down again and again. "Order. I'll have order in this courtroom," he bellowed. "I want a toasted sesame bagel with low-fat scallion cream cheese. You folks can order whatever you want, but get separate checks."

Robin Hood and Little John looked puzzled. "Your honor,

we would like to ask for a postponement," Robin Hood said as the family took whatever seats they could find. "We only just learned our client was being tried a half an hour ago."

"Your client wasn't tried a half an hour ago. He is being tried right now," the judge said matter-of-factly.

"No, your honor, I mean we learned about the trial a half an hour ago."

"What trial a half an hour ago? I think the two of you should be concerned with the trial that is going on right now!"

Little John looked as if he might climb up on the podium and strangle the judge, but Robin gestured for him to calm down. "Your honor. As I was saying, we wish to postpone this case until we've have had time to speak with our client about his defense, as well as to interview the prosecution's witnesses."

The judge's face turned beet-red and he slammed his hammer down, angrily. "Overruled!"

"But your honor—" Robin begged.

"Why did you invite us down here if you aren't ready for the trial?" the judge moaned.

"Sir, we didn't invite you down here," Little John protested.

"Well, that's terribly rude," the judge cried. "You put on a trial and you don't have the common decency to invite me? Counselors, you are not getting off to a good start."

"This guy acts like he's lost his mind," Sabrina said.

"He has," Granny whispered. "He's the Mad Hatter."

Sabrina's mouth fell open and she gaped at the judge in disbelief. Even she knew the story of the Mad Hatter. Alice met him at a tea party and he nearly drove the poor girl mental. He was the very definition of crazy.

"How did he get to be a judge?" Uncle Jake asked.

"I appointed him," a woman's voice said from behind them. Sabrina turned and found Mayor Heart sitting directly behind her. Heart's face was painted in bone-white pancake makeup, dark ruby lipstick, and purple eye shadow that crept up to the edge of her hairline. She looked like a deranged party clown— worse, she looked like Sabrina did when she tried to put on her own makeup.

"This isn't fair," Sabrina seethed. "You can't have a mental patient running a courtroom."

"As a matter of fact, I can. You see, I'm the mayor," Heart replied, then broke into a laugh. "Still, it doesn't matter who I appoint to oversee this case, brat. It will end the same way. The Wolf is going to swing from a rope and then there will be no one left to protect you."

A commotion at the front of the room turned Sabrina's attention back to the trial. "Where is the prosecuting attorney?" Judge Hatter asked.

"I'm right here, your honor," a man shouted as he barreled through the double doors into the courtroom. Sabrina took one look at him and cringed. She felt her sister's hand slip into her own. This man's beard, moustache, and hair were an unnatural shade of blue.

"Bluebeard." Uncle Jake gasped, along with most of the others in the courtroom.

"I'm quite ready to get started if it pleases the court," Bluebeard said as he stepped over to an empty desk and put down his briefcase. "In fact, I'm ready to call my first witness."

Robin Hood glared at Bluebeard. "I haven't had any time to discuss the case with my client. I haven't interviewed any of your witnesses."

"That's unfortunate," Bluebeard said. "But I have no doubt you'll catch up. As for right now, like I said, I'm ready to call my first witness. Rather, I have three witnesses, and I'd like to call them all to the stand at the same time, if it pleases the court."

"It might," Hatter said, clapping like a happy child. "Call your witnesses."

Robin pulled his partner back to the defendant's table. Once

Little John was calm, he and Robin tried to assure Mr. Canis that everything would be fine. The old man acted as if he couldn't hear them.

"The prosecution calls the Three Little Pigs to the stand," Bluebeard said. One of the card soldiers opened the double doors and in walked former deputies Boarman and Swineheart—two of the Three Little Pigs. They were both pear-shaped men, difficult to tell apart from a distance, but up close they had very distinct features. Jed Boarman had curly brown hair and wore glasses. He had a tiny little moustache, and he was prone to sweating profusely. His complexion was pale, even more so when walking into court, as he seemed quite nervous. His friend and business partner Alvin Swinehart had a pompadour haircut that reminded Sabrina of Elvis Presley. His long bushy sideburns and reflective sunglasses added to the resemblance. Both men were in ill-fitting suits and wearing ties. They scanned the courtroom as they entered and spotted Sabrina and her family, flashing them apologetic smiles that made Sabrina nervous. Were they going to say something that would hurt Mr. Canis's case?

Their arrival caused a great disturbance in the courtroom, and the gallery began to chatter. The noise made Hatter bang his forehead on his desktop and shout for order. Eventually, he remembered his hammer and slammed the tool down hard on the buckling wood instead. When the room was quiet, Bluebeard approached the men.

"I was under the impression that there were three of you."

Swineheart ran his hands through his slick black hair. "Well, there are, but we're not attached at the hip, ya know."

The crowd laughed until Hatter went to work with his hammer.

"So, am I to understand that Ernest Hamstead won't be joining us? Where is your friend?"

The men suddenly changed into pigs, a metamorphosis that occurred whenever they were nervous or excited. They honked and squealed for a moment but quickly reverted back to their human forms.

"We don't exactly know where he is," Boarman said sheepishly. "He's missing."

"Missing?" Bluebeard said. "How could someone go missing in a town this small?"

Boarman shrugged.

"I suppose the two of you will do," Bluebeard continued. "Gentlemen, will you tell us what you do for a living?"

"We're architects," Boarman said, "though not too long ago we were deputies for the Ferryport Landing Police Department."

"Fascinating," Bluebeard said. "According to the famous story of the three pigs, the three of you had a run in with the Big Bad Wolf. Is that correct?"

Boarman and Swineheart nodded.

"And if I've heard the story correctly, the three of you each built yourselves a home. One made a house out of straw, the other made a house of twigs, and the last—brick. Which one of you built which house?"

"I built the twig one," Swineheart said.

"And I built the brick," Boarman replied.

Bluebeard smiled and turned to the jury. "Now, I'm not a builder, but I know a thing or two about houses. You have to build them out of strong materials. Twigs are not going to pass building codes, but if you bribe the right official you might get away with it."

"I never bribed anyone in my life!" Swineheart cried.

Bluebeard ignored him. "But bricks are a pretty good building material. However, very few people would choose to build a house out of straw, would they?"

Boarman and Swineheart said nothing.

"Straw would fall down at the slightest wind. Straw would fall apart at the first rain. I could break into a straw house with a lawn mower!" Bluebeard shouted, causing a large portion of the gallery to chuckle. "But I'm no architect. Perhaps there's

something to this straw house. Tell me what happened to those houses."

Swineheart rolled his eyes impatiently. "The Wolf came along and blew two of them down. The brick house survived."

"He blew two of these houses down! How frightening! Do you see this wolf in the courtroom today?" Bluebeard asked. He turned to face Mr. Canis and a victorious smile crept across his face.

"Nope," said the pigs.

Bluebeard's face fell. "I'm sorry, gentlemen," he said. "Perhaps you didn't hear me correctly. I asked the two of you if either of you saw the Wolf in the courtroom."

"We know," Boarman said. "The answer was no."

Sabrina's head was swimming with questions. She knew the story of the pigs well. She also knew that Mr. Canis had been the one to destroy their homes. Were the pigs lying for him?

"You don't see the Wolf?" Bluebeard asked as he pointed at Mr. Canis.

Swineheart puffed up his chest and grinned. "That ain't the Wolf. That's a fellow we know by the name of Mr. Canis."

"Don't play games with me!" Bluebeard bellowed and slammed his fist down on this table. "The Wolf and Mr. Canis are the same person."

"No, you're wrong," Boarman added. "They aren't the same person. Mr. Canis is the man; the Wolf is a monster locked up inside him. If you put Mr. Canis on trial for crimes the Wolf committed, you're punishing the wrong man."

The audience erupted into babble but quickly stopped when Judge Hatter tossed his hammer through a window.

"Fine, let me ask you this," Bluebeard pressed. "Would the two of you characterize yourselves as friends of the Wolf . . . I mean Mr. Canis?"

"Well, sure," Boarman said.

"We're not hanging out at the ice-cream parlor together, but I'd say we have a lot of respect for him. We've helped one another in the past," Swineheart explained.

"Would you say Ernest Hamstead was friends with Mr. Canis?"

"Ernest was very close with Relda Grimm," Boarman continued. "He spent a lot more time with Canis. I think he'd come to trust him. I'd say they were good friends."

"So your missing friend, Ernest Hamstead, and Mr. Canis were chummy. This Mr. Hamstead is an interesting fellow. He built a house out of straw and was surprised at how easily it was demolished. He also came to befriend the monster that destroyed his property and tried to eat him. He sounds very trusting." Bluebeard turned to face Mr. Canis. "Maybe a little too trusting. Tell me, monster, were you truly friends with the pigs or have you been biding your time, waiting for the day when you could finish the diabolical work you started with a huff and a puff?'"

Mr. Canis snarled.

"Let's face it. Hamstead doesn't sound like the sharpest knife in the drawer. Did you finally see the opportunity to kill the dumbest of the bunch and feast on his bones? Did you kill and eat Mr. Hamstead like you did Little Red Riding Hood's defenseless old grandmother?"

"Objection!" Robin Hood shouted. "Mr. Canis is not on trial for killing Mr. Hamstead. There is no proof that Hamstead is even dead. Where is the body? Where is the murder weapon?"

"The murder weapon is the savage teeth on this brute!" Bluebeard shouted. "And the body is probably slowly digesting in his belly!"

Mr. Canis roared with rage. He swatted at the table in front of him, knocking it against a wall. It crumbled into splinters. A dozen card soldiers appeared and sprang on Canis. They clubbed him with the hilts of their swords, but their blows didn't seem to faze him. Sabrina watched in horror. She had never seen Mr. Canis lose his temper so quickly. He tore into the guards like they were nothing, bellowing savagely. Eventually, reinforcements arrived, and the soldiers managed to drag Canis from the courtroom.

Judge Hatter, who had been wildly hammering with his fists, slumped in his chair and wiped his face with his robe. "We've heard enough for today. We'll meet back here Tuesday."

"But your honor," Bluebeard said. "Tuesday was yesterday."

"Hmmm . . . you may be right. When would you like to meet, again?"

"Tomorrow?"

"My good man, you're a genius. We can't exactly begin yesterday can we? No, really, can we?"

Bluebeard shook his head.

"Very well, time marches on despite our best efforts. We shall meet tomorrow," Judge Hatter said.

"But your honor!" Little John cried. "We haven't had an opportunity to question the witnesses."

Unfortunately, the judge ignored the big man's protest and darted out of the room. The Five of Diamonds dismissed the crowd and they began to file out through the double doors. As she left, Sabrina caught Mayor Heart squinting at her. The nasty woman was giggling like an idiot and flashing her yellow and crooked teeth. "Better luck tomorrow," she cackled.

Sabrina watched Robin Hood deflate. He looked around the

court, bewildered and mystified. "What just happened?" he asked.

"We got steamrolled, that's what happened," Little John grumbled.

• • •

The family hadn't been home ten minutes before there was a knock at the door. When Sabrina answered it, she found Swineheart and Boarman standing on the porch looking embarrassed.

"We know you didn't have a choice," Granny said after Sabrina invited the two men inside.

"We still feel like we let him down," Swineheart said.

"I'm sure Mr. Canis knows you were trying to help," Granny assured them. She brought them both tall glasses of iced tea and had them sit at the dining room table while she went to prepare snacks.

"This trial is a travesty," Boarman complained. "We can't let them get away with this!"

"I don't know how we're going to stop them," Sabrina said. "Mayor Heart handpicked the judge, and there are several members of the Scarlet Hand on the jury."

"Perhaps the two of you might be interested in helping us," Granny said as she entered the dining room with a plate full of roast beef sandwiches, along with sauerkraut, pickles, baked beans, and egg salad. Sabrina couldn't believe how normal the lunch was. She was going to have to invite people in more often.

"Help?" Swineheart said as he eyed the sandwiches hungrily.

"With our defense," Granny said. "Today, they caught us off guard, and we can't let that happen again. I believe the key to our success is preparation. We need to read everything we can about Red Riding Hood, her grandmother, Mr. Canis, and anything else related to the crime. Unfortunately, there are hundreds of versions of the Red Riding Hood story. You two have known Canis a lot longer than us, and I think you might be good at weeding out the facts from the fiction."

Boarman and Swineheart nodded.

"We'll do our best," Boarman said, "right after we have one of those delicious sandwiches."

Granny Relda gave the pigs two sandwiches each and let them eat as much as they wanted of the other dishes. Sabrina had never seen anyone eat as much as the two former deputies. They shoveled food into their mouths and were eager for more moments later. While they ate they went to work sifting through the family's countless books. Sabrina, Daphne, Uncle Jake, and Granny helped search.

"What should we be looking for?" Daphne said.

"Any kind of discrepancy," Granny replied.

Daphne took out her pocket dictionary. That she didn't just ask Sabrina was infuriating. It was easy enough to tell her sister that *discrepancy* was another word for *contradiction,* but the little girl didn't seem to want Sabrina's help anymore. It hurt her to feel that "grown-up" Daphne no longer needed her.

"I don't even know what we're supposed to be looking for," Sabrina grumbled as she flipped through the books. "It was six hundred years ago."

"Well, we should read them all, anyway," Daphne said. "Maybe we'll find that there were other eyewitnesses."

"I think all the eyewitnesses are in the Wolf's belly," Sabrina said.

Granny flashed her an angry look. The old woman still had not said anything directly to her since their spat the day before.

The group went through as many books as the afternoon would allow, but Sabrina's heart was not in the research. The memory of Canis in the courtroom kept popping into her head. His rage-filled eyes and horrible roar made her shudder. Was there anything human left in her grandmother's friend, and if so, how long could it hold out against the monster? Even more unsettling was her family's lack of worry. What if the Wolf were to escape his chains in court, or overpower Nottingham and bust out of jail? Would he come back to Granny's house? What would the Grimms do if he showed up at their front door? What would they do if he lost his temper with them? It seemed as if she was the only one considering the dark possibilities.

While everyone was searching through the books, she managed to catch Boarman and Swineheart in the kitchen, rummaging in the refrigerator for more sandwiches. She carefully closed the kitchen door behind her, making double sure that no one was listening, and then turned to the men.

"Mr. Hamstead is alive," she said.

"We know," Swineheart said. "He wrote us a letter. You know the next time you folks leave town and want to bring along an Everafter, don't hesitate to call."

"Sorry," Sabrina said. "It was a last-minute thing. He also gave us the key."

The men shared a nervous look.

"He didn't tell us that," Boarman said. "Has your grandmother retrieved the weapon yet?"

Sabrina shook her head. "No, he gave the key to Daphne and me. He told us not to go get the weapon until we absolutely have to, but the way Mr. Canis is looking, I'd say it's high time. Mr. Hamstead said you two could teach us how to use it."

"What's to know?" Boarman said. "It's pretty self-explanatory. Just don't point it at anything you don't mean to destroy."

Swineheart chuckled. "You remember when Ernest aimed it at his new car? I heard they found it in the next county."

The pigs burst into laughter, both turning bright red before they got themselves under control.

"We shouldn't laugh," Boarman said. "His insurance premiums went through the roof. Still, we had to try it out before we used it on ol' furball's behind."

"You three were the only ones to beat the Wolf, right? Mr. Hamstead told us a little and I've heard others mention it before, but I've never heard exactly what happened," Sabrina asked.

Swineheart sighed. "Well, back before you were born the Wolf marched through this town terrorizing people, and no one could stop him. Not even your Grandpa Basil could control him, and Basil was one of the smartest and toughest human beings I ever met. Naturally, a furry lunatic running around blowing people's houses down is the responsibility of the police department, but there was little we could do. We organized a posse from time to time, got people together to search for his den. I even had a witch fly me over the forest, hoping I would spot him from the air. All of it was a major waste of time. He was too smart and fast, and sadly, the savagery continued."

"This drove Mayor Charming crazy," Boarman added. "He said we looked foolish, and worse, we wasted taxpayer money. He always thought he was the answer to everyone's problems so he went out looking himself. When we found him a week later, he was hanging upside down from a tree. The Wolf had tied him up with his own rope. Charming was humiliated."

"That explains why Charming and Canis never liked each other," Sabrina said.

Boarman nodded. "When we cut him down, Charming gave us a mandate: Stop the Wolf or stop coming to work. So we put our heads together. We tried to trap him, shoot him with tranquilizer darts, even poison him, but he was always a step ahead of us. Then it dawned on me that the Wolf wasn't playing fair. Sure, he was a tough hombre on his own but he was using this magic weapon, too. It made him unstoppable. The second you got close to him, he'd turn it on you and bam! Game over! So, it seemed obvious to me that we had to get it away from him first."

"Obvious to *you*, huh?" Swineheart said.

"Fine! We all came up with this idea," Boarman surrendered. "The point is we had to get it away from him, and to do that we had to trick him. We spread the word that Old McDonald was concerned about how big his flock of sheep had gotten. We knew the stories of the Wolf and how much he enjoyed eating sheep, so we sat in the barn and waited for him. It wasn't long before he showed up."

"Unfortunately, we were dressed as sheep."

"I was going to leave out the embarrassing parts of the story," Boarman groaned.

"Don't candycoat it," Swineheart said. "It all turned out OK. Suffice it to say, the Wolf never saw us coming. When he stormed into the barn I hit him with a pickup truck."

"You ran him over?" Sabrina gasped.

"I had to!" Swineheart said. "He's huge and mean. If I had had a tank I would have driven over him. Luckily, the truck knocked the Wolf off his feet long enough for Hamstead to drop from the ceiling and scoop up the weapon. You should have seen it, kid. We were like three fat little ninjas. Hamstead swooped down on a rope. Boarman smacked him with a shovel. I gunned the engine. It was a big day for pigs everywhere."

"And then you turned the weapon on him?"

"Heck no," Boarman said. "We ran."

"Wee-wee-wee, all the way home." Swineheart laughed. "We had to. I'd never seen the big guy so mad. We hopped in our squad cars and hightailed it out of there. He chased us all over Ferryport Landing before he finally gave up."

Boarman grinned from ear to ear. "Once we had the weapon, we practiced a few times, destroyed a little property accidentally, and prepared for the big showdown with the furball. The Wolf didn't disappoint. He charged into the police station with his teeth and claws, looking to turn us all into pork chops, but he got the beating of his life. I'm telling you, kid—the Three Little Pigs laid the smackdown on his fuzzy behind."

"But when the smoke cleared there was something none of us had expected," Swineheart said. He took off his sunglasses, rubbed a smudge with his shirt, and put them back on.

"What? Was it the weapon? Did it break or something?" Sabrina demanded, praying that the device was still intact.

"Oh, no, the weapon was just fine. It's just, well—we got a big surprise."

"What?"

"Mr. Canis," Boarman said.

"I'm confused," Sabrina said.

"So were we. Still are to a certain degree," Boarman explained. "All I know is that there was no such person as Mr. Canis before that fight. We didn't know he existed until that moment. Maybe it was the weapon, maybe we just beat him so bad he split into another person, but when all was said and done there was no Wolf, only Mr. Canis, all gray-haired and skinny.

"Poor guy didn't have any memories of who he was. He didn't even know that he had once been a monster—he was like a full-grown man who seemed to sprout up out of the dust. We took him to your grandfather. Basil had a lot of experience with stuff like that, but it was Relda who took it upon herself to help him. Soon they discovered that Canis could tap into the Wolf's power, and even better, he had control over the monster. Relda told me she thought that Canis could be a great ally, and he's been living with your family ever since. For fifteen years we've all slept a little easier. I don't know why he lost control, but it happened around the time you girls moved to town."

Sabrina knew exactly what had happened. Canis and Jack the Giant Killer had come to blows and in the fight Canis had tasted Jack's blood. After that, the bloodlust seemed to collapse the walls between their family friend and the monster inside him. Sabrina had never suspected how long those walls had taken to build.

"So, this weapon will stop the Wolf, but could it—"

"Give Mr. Canis control, again?" Swineheart interrupted. "It might."

"And what is it? What is this weapon?"

Just then, Granny entered the kitchen with a tray of dirty dishes. "Oh, dear. I had no idea there was anyone in here. I'm afraid that we're losing our little team. Jacob fell asleep an hour ago and Daphne just dozed off herself. Gentlemen, why don't you two call it a night as well? We appreciate everything you've done."

"Our pleasure," the men assured her.

"Sabrina, why don't you help your sister into bed while I say good-bye to our friends?" Granny asked.

Sabrina was eager to learn more about the weapon but she knew the time for questions was over for the night. She said her good-byes and went searching for her sister.

Daphne was asleep on the sofa. She gently shook her and the girl woke enough to walk upstairs. Once they were in their room, Sabrina took off her sister's clothes and pearl necklace and helped her into her pajamas. A vial of Sabrina's lip gloss slipped out of Daphne's purse and rolled across the floor. Sabrina frowned and scooped it up. She pulled the covers up to her sister's elbows and turned off her bedside table lamp.

"You comfy?" she asked the sleepy girl.

Daphne mumbled something unintelligible. Moments later, the little girl was sound asleep and snoring.

Sabrina lay there watching her little sister. A sliver of silver shined in Sabrina's eyes. The moonlight was reflecting off the tiny key around Daphne's neck.

• • •

For the second morning in a row, everyone was woken by a loud banging on the front door. Sabrina hurried out of bed and down the stairs, smoothing her hair as she went and wishing Robin Hood wasn't such an early riser. But when she stepped into the hallway, she heard her uncle, who had beaten her downstairs, cry, "It's here! It's here!" to the gathering group.

"What's here?" Daphne asked the others.

Granny shrugged.

Uncle Jake opened the door and on the other side was a small spotted rabbit wearing a blue jacket and matching ball cap. His shirt had a company logo that read THD TORTOISE AND HARE DELIVERIES WORLDWIDE. Under his little arm he held a clipboard and ink pen and next to him on the porch was an immense wooden chest sitting on the back of a large green tortoise.

When Daphne saw the animals, she squealed. "You are so cute I could eat you!" she cried, but when she saw Sabrina's amused smile, she straightened her face. "I mean . . . I'm pleased to meet you."

"You Jake Grimm?" the rabbit squeaked.

"Yes," Uncle Jake said.

"You gotta sign for this," the rabbit said, gesturing toward the delivery.

Uncle Jake took the clipboard, found his name, and signed it.

"What you got in this thing, anyway?" the tortoise asked. "It weighs a ton."

"Oh, this and that," Uncle Jake replied.

The rabbit held out his paw and stared up at the family.

"Well, thanks for bringing it by," Uncle Jake replied.

The rabbit and the tortoise didn't budge.

"I guess you probably have other deliveries to make," Uncle Jake continued.

"Listen, pal. Let's not beat around the bush. It's customary to tip for a delivery, especially a backbreaking shipment like this. We brought this thing all the way from the truck and we got it here fast. I could have had my partner deliver it but you wouldn't have gotten it until next year. You know how long a tortoise takes to deliver a package?"

"Long time, pal," the tortoise said.

"Real long time. That kind of express service deserves a little tip, don't you think? I mean, I got a big family. Really, I'm talking big. So how about throwing me a couple extra bills?"

"Of course," Uncle Jake said, digging in his pockets. He pulled out a wadded five-dollar bill and stuffed it into the rabbit's shirt pocket. Then he took the chest off the tortoise's back.

"Thanks, pal. Oh, there's one more thing," the rabbit said as he took off his ball cap. There he had hidden a long brass key, which he handed to Uncle Jake. "Have a nice day and remember to use THD. We get it there at any speed you need." The rabbit turned, snatched the back legs of the tortoise like he was a wheelbarrow, and headed back to their truck.

"What's this?" Granny asked.

"You'll see," Uncle Jake said. "Get dressed and meet me in the Mirror's room." When they joined him ten minutes later they found him standing in front of the chest. "So, girls, remember when we started looking for Goldilocks and I suggested we send her a letter?"

The girls nodded.

"Well, I realized early on that we weren't going to be able to do that," Uncle Jake said. "Goldilocks keeps moving from one place to the next, faster than we could ever get a letter to her. So, I called a few friends for some help and they sent me this."

"What is it?" Sabrina asked.

"It's a traveler's chest," Uncle Jake said.

"A traveler's what?" Sabrina asked.

"Where did you get this?" Granny Relda asked as she looked at the chest. "Your father used to talk about these, but I always thought he was pulling my leg."

"The Andersen triplets loaned it to us. It's going to help us find Goldilocks," Uncle Jake said. "At least that's what they told me it will do."

Sabrina examined the chest. "How does it work?"

Uncle Jake took the brass key and opened the lock on the front of the chest. He lifted the lid, but the box was completely empty.

"An old empty chest is going to help us find Goldilocks?" Daphne asked.

"Oops," Uncle Jake said as he closed the lid. "I forgot to tell it where I wanted to go."

"I'm confused," Daphne said.

"All you have to do is tell the chest where you want to travel. Watch!" Uncle Jake said. "Chest, I'm traveling to the Hotel Cipriani at Guidecca 10 in Venice, Italy."

Sabrina and Daphne stared at their uncle, then looked at each other.

"I think he's finally lost it," Daphne said.

"It was bound to happen," Sabrina added.

"Ha! You want to see?" Jake cried. He turned the key in the lock and lifted the lid. Instead of an empty box, Sabrina saw a spiral staircase and immediately felt the familiar tingle of an enchanted item.

"Daphne first," Uncle Jake said as he helped the girl onto

the staircase. Daphne looked up at Granny Relda as if she were unsure of what to do, but Granny's nod gave her permission to go. Sabrina went next, followed by Uncle Jake.

"Mom, want to come along?"

Sabrina could see her grandmother's nervous face over the edge of the chest. "No, one of us has to stay here," the old lady said. "Besides, I'm going to bake some muffins and take them to Robin and Little John."

"Be careful," Uncle Jake said.

Granny promised she would, then backed out of view.

Sabrina examined the inside of the chest. The light was dim and grew dimmer as they descended. When they found themselves in pure darkness, Uncle Jake took a small red amulet from one of his jacket pockets. He whispered something into it, and it lit up their path. They continued down, step after step, until Sabrina was convinced there was no bottom. She was about to suggest they turn back when she heard her sister bang into something. From her groan, it sounded as if it was something quite hard.

"Could someone have warned me there would be a door down here?" Daphne complained.

"Sorry," Uncle Jake said. "You can open it, but don't step out until you've looked both ways. These traveler's chests have a tendency to be imprecise, and that door is leading into the real world. Anything could be on the other side."

Daphne opened the door and looked to her left, then her right. "Looks all clear!" she said, stepping through the opening. A moment later, Sabrina heard a huge splash and Daphne's cries for help.

5

abrina rushed through the door. There she found her sister bobbing up and down in a canal. She nearly fell into it herself, but Uncle Jake pulled her back just in time.

Several men in white pants and shirts were standing in long, thin boats they maneuvered down the waterway using tall poles. One used his pole to nudge Daphne to the side of the canal, where Uncle Jake fished her out.

When she was safely back on land, she reached into her pocket for her dictionary, but the book was waterlogged and ruined. Her face crinkled up in frustration, and she tossed it into a nearby trash can. "What does *imprecise* mean?" Daphne snapped.

"It means *not exact*," Sabrina said.

Daphne scowled.

"You should have asked before," Sabrina said.

Daphne scowled harder, then emptied the water from her shoes.

"Welcome to Venice, girls," Uncle Jake said.

Sabrina studied her surroundings. Scarecrow had been correct. There weren't streets in Venice, at least not in the part of the city where they were. Instead, the neighborhoods seemed to be connected by an elaborate canal system lined by narrow sidewalks. The elegant hotels, office buildings, and apartments on either side of the canals were built high so that doorways never touched the water. Boats of various shapes and sizes sailed by: some were taxis, and others were for tourists to take on romantic rides through the majestic arches and bridges of Venice. As a native New Yorker, Sabrina was rarely impressed with anything outside of the Big Apple. After all, once a person had seen the Statue of Liberty or had one of Nathan's hot dogs at Coney Island, there was little reason to see the rest of the world. But she had to admit Venice was awe-inspiring.

"So, where's Goldilocks?" Sabrina said, pulling her attention away from the amazing scenery and back to the group. She noticed her uncle seemed to be hypnotized by something. He was looking up at the third floor of a hotel across the canal.

"There," he said, pointing at a beautiful woman standing on the balcony. She had tight blond curls, a sun-kissed tan, and a warm smile. She, too, was gazing out at the amazing city.

Sabrina was overwhelmed, unsure of whether to laugh or cry. For months she and Daphne had thought their parents abandoned them, only to find out they had been kidnapped. Rescuing them had provided little comfort since they were both victims of a magical spell. Now that obstacle was almost hurdled, too. Hope, wonder, and joy were building in her heart, threatening to explode like a shaken bottle of soda pop. The feelings were mirrored in the faces of her family as well. Daphne, despite being soaked, was grinning ear to ear. Uncle Jake's fatigue seemed to melt away as he waved for the girls to follow him.

They crossed a bridge to get to the hotel and rushed into the busy lobby. The Hotel Cipriani was even more impressive than the Scarecrow had led them to believe. The floors were made from priceless marble. Opulent arches framed the doors and beautiful sculptures decorated the lobby. The ceiling hung so high above them, Sabrina wondered if clouds ever drifted into the hotel. Dozens of bellhops rushed to and fro, carrying expensive luggage and helping guests to their rooms. Unfortunately, the group's arrival did not go unnoticed and a chubby, gray-haired man in a black suit approached them. His face was full of disapproval. Sabrina realized how odd they looked for such an elegant place, her sister dripping wet and her uncle in his wrinkled blue jeans and bizarre overcoat.

"*Posso aiutarvi?*" he said.

"I'm sorry, we don't speak Italian," Uncle Jake said.

His comment caused the man's frown lines to deepen. "Americans," he huffed. "Are you lost?"

"No, we're looking for a guest of the hotel," Uncle Jake said.

"What is this guest's name?"

"Well, this is going to sound silly, but her name is Goldilocks," Sabrina said, bracing herself for a laugh. However, the man didn't even blink.

"You are friends with Ms. Locks?" he said.

Uncle Jake nodded. "Yes, we're very close."

The hotel manager seemed reluctant.

"Listen pal," Uncle Jake said, "are you going to help us find her or should we just start knocking on doors?"

The man's eyes widened in horror. "Take the elevators along the east wall. She's on the third floor—suite 311."

"Thank you," Daphne said.

The group took an elevator to the third floor and followed the hallways until they found the room.

"This is it," Daphne said, taking Sabrina's hand. "I can't wait to talk to Mom and Dad. They're going to be surprised by how much we've grown."

"You want to do the honors?" Uncle Jake asked her, gesturing to the door.

Sabrina nodded. She took a deep breath and knocked on the door. It drifted open at her touch. The lock and doorjamb were splintered and broken.

The Grimms looked at one another, suspicious. Uncle Jake frowned, pulled a magic wand from his overcoat, and stepped through the doorway. Nothing else seemed to be disturbed in the front room, but there were doors leading to others.

"Hello?" Jake called out.

There was no answer, but a moment later Sabrina heard the sound of breaking glass. Uncle Jake held up his hand to motion for everyone to be quiet. They heard a door slam and followed the sound, walking through the beautiful suite filled with elegant furniture, paintings, and linens. When they got to a closed door, their uncle turned the doorknob and pushed the door open. "Goldie? Are you OK?"

Just then, a tall man in a black jacket and pants appeared from behind the door. He was wearing a black motorcycle helmet that disguised his identity. On his chest was a horrible mark: a handprint in red paint. The paint ran down in drips like blood. The girls had seen the mark many times, but never so far from home. It was the mark of the Scarlet Hand.

The mysterious man punched Uncle Jake hard in the face and

pushed past the girls and out of the room. As soon as he was gone, Sabrina and Daphne helped their uncle to his feet.

"That wasn't very cool," her uncle complained as he rubbed his jaw.

"Who was that?" Sabrina asked.

"Beats me," Uncle Jake said.

"Where's Goldilocks?"

They searched the other rooms but there was no sign of the blond beauty, or anyone else for that matter.

"I think she left in a hurry," Uncle Jake said. "Her clothes and suitcase are still in the closet."

Suddenly, Sabrina heard a loud engine start. Everyone rushed out to the balcony to find its source. The masked villain was on the narrow sidewalk below the hotel, sitting atop a black motorcycle. He revved his engine, sending a loud rumbling throughout the neighborhood, then sped along the edge of the canal. Sabrina wondered where he was racing until she spotted Goldilocks drifting down the waterway in a gondola. The motorcyclist was following her.

"She's in trouble," Daphne said.

"C'mon!" Uncle Jake cried and led the children out into the hall. They bypassed the elevator for the faster stairs. They ran through the lobby, causing the manager to cross his arms with a harrumph, and then they charged through the front doors out into the city. Outside, Sabrina spotted Goldilocks. She was surprised at the distance the boat had traveled in such a short time.

"What now?" she asked, but Daphne had already sprung into action. She descended a flight of wooden steps and jumped into an empty gondola. A moment later, she had the barge pole and was pushing away from the dock, giving the rest of the group only seconds to climb aboard. Uncle Jake took the pole and after a few awkward attempts, the group was floating down the canal in pursuit of the beautiful woman. Sabrina heard angry shouts from behind them and turned to see a red-faced gondolier race to the steps and shake his fist at the boat and its occupants.

Daphne waved at the man apologetically. "Sorry! This is an emergency."

Uncle Jake pushed harder and harder with the pole, trying to catch up with Goldilocks. All the while, the man on the motorcycle puttered along like a mechanical tiger stalking its lunch. When he ran out of sidewalk he simply steered onto one of the city's beautiful bridges and crossed to the other side of the street. His erratic behavior turned the heads of tourists and locals alike, as the sidewalks were built for pedestrians only. On more than one occasion he forced an unlucky person to leap into the water to avoid being run over. The commotion was causing problems in the canal, too. Boats steered out of the way to avoid colliding with the unexpected swimmers. Other boats stopped abruptly, causing a traffic jam. In a matter of seconds, the family's chase had come to a complete halt.

"What do we do now?" Sabrina said, watching Goldilocks's boat at the head of the line. She was still drifting along undeterred.

Uncle Jake set the pole in the boat. "We improvise," he said, stepping onto the boat next to theirs. Daphne was right behind him, followed by Sabrina. They moved from one boat to the next, careful not to capsize each new vessel. Soon they were making good progress and closing the gap between themselves and Goldilocks.

Daphne called out to the woman when they were just three boats away. Goldilocks turned to them, but her attention was quickly distracted. The motorcyclist in black raced up a bridge directly over the canal and parked his bike. The bridge was under construction, and several large stones intended for the repairs were stacked nearby. The motorcyclist heaved one off the bridge and onto Goldilocks' boat. His aim was either incredible or incredibly lucky. The heavy stone blasted through the bottom of the boat and water started pouring through the hole like a geyser. Startled, the gondolier leaped into the water, leaving Goldilocks to fend for herself.

Goldilocks, however, stood up calmly, glanced around as if searching for someone, and then did something so odd that Sabrina wondered if the woman was insane. She began chirping and squawking at a pigeon resting on the bridge. The bird seemed just as surprised by the woman's noises as Sabrina, and it flew into the air.

"What was that all about?" Sabrina asked, but before anyone could answer, a flock of pigeons returned, casting an enormous shadow over the canal. They dove down to Goldilocks's boat and dug their tiny talons into her clothes. Together they lifted her out of the boat, their wings flapping furiously. Goldilocks sailed high above the canals and over the hotels and other buildings. Sabrina gaped as she watched the woman disappear into the horizon.

"Did you see that? It was like she was talking to those birds. They seemed to understand her!" Sabrina said.

"Yeah, I forgot about that," Uncle Jake said. "Goldilocks can talk to animals."

Sabrina scanned the bridge for the motorcyclist but he was gone. All she heard was the sound of his engine fading in the distance.

"Who was that guy, anyway?" Daphne asked as their boat bumped into the gondola of some Japanese honeymooners.

"I don't know," Uncle Jake said. "But now I know why Goldie keeps moving around so much. He's chasing her. She's in danger."

• • •

When the family returned home, there was no time to relax or even discuss what had just happened. Granny Relda and Barto the miniature orc were waiting. Judge Hatter had moved the trial up by three hours. If they didn't leave for the courthouse right away they would miss the day's proceedings. Granny ushered them all downstairs and into the family car. Uncle Jake started the massive jalopy, and after a good ten minutes of knocks and rattles, and several loud backfires, the vehicle was on the road headed toward the courthouse.

The courtroom was more packed than the day before with many fresh faces in the crowd.

"Stay close, people," Barto insisted as he eyed the spectators suspiciously. Sabrina watched her sister roll her eyes at the little security guard, but said nothing. Her attention was focused on Snow White, whom she spotted near the door. Ms. White smiled when they entered and Sabrina waved at her. Granny thanked her for coming, though their conversation was short and stiff. Even Briar Rose was there. She kissed Uncle Jake on the cheek, and he returned the gesture by kissing the palm of her hand. They all squeezed into seats.

Robin and Little John had warned them that the trial would be more difficult the second day, and they weren't kidding. Bluebeard continued his prosecution of Mr. Canis by calling witnesses that had been victimized by the Wolf hundreds of years before. There was a steady stream of talking lambs, pigs, and assorted forest creatures. Little Bo Peep, complete with staff and flock, complained that she hadn't actually lost her sheep but that the Wolf had eaten them. And just as he had done the previous day, Judge Hatter refused to allow Robin and Little John a chance to ask their own questions. Nottingham and Mayor Heart watched the proceedings with amused expressions, openly cackling whenever the family's lawyers were prevented from defending Mr. Canis.

The day dragged on, and by late afternoon, Sabrina wondered if there was a citizen left in Ferryport Landing whom the Wolf had not tried to devour. She watched Canis, waiting for an outburst from him. If he were to escape, there would be nothing Nottingham and the mayor's card soldiers could do to stop him.

"Does the prosecution have any more witnesses today?" Judge Hatter asked.

"We are finished for today, your honor," Bluebeard said.

Robin leaped up. "We have a few witnesses we'd like to question."

"Very well," Judge Hatter said as he got to his feet. "Let's meet in the morning." He strolled out of the courtroom, oblivious to Robin and Little John's angry shouts.

"This is outrageous!" Little John bellowed, knocking over his chair and startling many of the onlookers. Nottingham, standing nearby, laughed heartily.

"Yes, it is, isn't it?" the sheriff said cheerfully.

Little John looked like he might lunge at Nottingham, but Robin Hood held him back. "He's not worth the headache, my large friend."

Nottingham laughed even harder as he joined Mayor Heart, and together they left the courtroom. The crowd of onlookers started to follow, and Bluebeard rushed forward, shoving people out of his way. He grabbed Snow White by the wrist before she could leave. Sabrina couldn't hear what he was saying to her, but Ms. White looked nervous and pale. Daphne noticed them talking, too, as, clearly, did the jury member in the black-hooded cloak. Though Sabrina could still not make out his face, he hovered on the edges of the crowd, obviously trying to listen to the villain and the beautiful teacher.

"What should we do?" Daphne said.

"Don't worry," Barto said. He took out his walkie-talkie and barked a couple of orders into it. A moment later, a battalion of little green trolls raced into the room, surrounded Bluebeard, and tackled him. Bluebeard fell to the ground and swatted at them viciously, but there were too many for him to overpower. Taking advantage of the distraction, Snow snuck out of the courtroom, but not before she turned to the family and mouthed the words *thank you.*

When she was safely gone, Sabrina turned to Barto, whose chest was puffed up with pride. "I owe you one," the girl exclaimed.

"Just doing my job," Barto said. "Though, if you felt it appropriate to mention this to Puck, I'd be most grateful, I would."

Now that Snow was gone, the juror in the black cloak had vanished as well. Sabrina turned her attention back to her grandmother, who was busy trying to reassure Robin and Little John.

"You're doing your best."

"Our best is not going to keep your friend alive," Little John grunted.

"I agree," Robin said. "We're going to have to change our game plan."

"How so?" Uncle Jake asked.

"If they won't let us question their witnesses in court, I think we should ask them questions outside of court," Robin said. "If only we knew who some of the eyewitnesses were."

"Eyewitnesses?" Sabrina asked. "It was six hundred years ago."

Granny's face suddenly blanched. "There's at least one eyewitness I know."

"Mom," Uncle Jake said. "You don't mean—"

"Aww, no!" Daphne cried. "Not the nutcase."

Granny nodded. "We need to go talk to Red Riding Hood."

• • •

After her "pet" Jabberwocky had attacked the town, Red Riding Hood had been hospitalized in the mental-health wing of the Ferryport Landing Memorial Hospital. Even an irresponsible lunatic like the town's mayor, the Queen of Hearts, knew that Red Riding Hood was too dangerous to be allowed to roam free. Heart had consulted some witches, who had put a magical barrier around Red's room. It allowed the girl to receive doctors, nurses, and any visitors brave enough to come near her, but it prevented Red from leaving. Sabrina didn't have a lot of faith in the spell. Red had managed to escape a similar one before with disastrous results.

When the group arrived, Sabrina sensed the jittery hospital staff shared her nervousness. There were only a few people working in Red's wing but they all looked tired, with dark circles under their eyes and unkempt hair. The slightest noise sent a few nurses into hysterics. It didn't help matters that besides Red, the hospital was completely empty. Since most of the humans from Ferryport Landing had been run out of town, there was no one who needed medical care. Everafters never got sick, and when they were injured they healed very fast without the need for bandages and prescriptions. Red's insane screams echoing down the lonely halls made the hospital very creepy.

A nurse met them at the door. She looked exhausted. Deep lines had formed in the corners of her chubby mouth and her eyes were almost vacant, as if someone had turned the light off behind them. In addition, Sabrina had never seen a woman as fat as Nurse Sprat. She suspected the woman weighed upward of eight hundred pounds. She had also never seen a nurse eat a foot-long roast beef sandwich while she was on duty.

"The child is quite popular this week," Nurse Sprat said between bites. "You're her second group of visitors in the same amount of days."

"Bluebeard," Robin Hood said.

Nurse Sprat nodded. "Creepy guy. He and Red are like two peas in a pod. He was in her room for hours asking questions."

"Did you hear what any of them were?" Little John asked.

"Nope. Truth is, I stay as far away from the patient as possible. She's what we in the medical profession call a loopty-loop."

"We're aware of her troubles. What kind of treatment are you using on her? Drugs? Therapy? Counseling?" Robin asked.

"Treatment?" Nurse Sprat asked. "She's completely off her rocker. There's no treatment for a brain like hers. Poor thing. The things she's seen. I'd probably have a couple screws loose, too, if I saw my grandmother get eaten."

Nurse Sprat led them down a long, sterile hallway and stopped outside of a doorway that read MEDICAL PERSONNEL ONLY. The door had a dozen heavy-duty locks and a metal bar across it. Obviously, the staff had as little faith in the barrier spell as Sabrina did.

"She's right in there, folks," the nurse said, and she went about unlocking the door. When she was finished she opened it and stepped aside.

"You're not going in with us?" Granny Relda asked.

"No way. She gives me the heebie-jeebies. But if I hear you screaming, I promise I'll come running."

"Thanks," Sabrina grumbled.

"By the way," Nurse Sprat said as she waddled back down the hall. "Keep your fingers in your pockets. She's a biter."

"Perhaps I should guard the door," Barto said as he peered into Red's room.

Robin Hood led the group into a bright white room with prison bars on the windows. Crayons and colored pencils were scattered about, many smashed underfoot and smeared on the room's marble floor. Thousands of drawings were taped to the walls, all depicting the same scene: a small house in the woods surrounded by a mother, father, grandmother, a dog, and a small girl in a red cloak. The mother was carrying a baby in her arms.

Red Riding Hood sat at a tiny pink table bolted to the floor. She was having a tea party with several stuffed dolls. All the dolls were mangled and beaten. Most were missing their eyes, others legs and arms.

"Party guests!" Red Riding Hood cried, clapping her hands and laughing. "Please, do have a seat. There's plenty of tea."

"Relda, if you'd like to ask the questions, feel free," Little John said, eyeing the girl nervously.

"Of course," Granny said. "I've had some experience with Red."

"Yeah, like that time she tried to kidnap you and kill us," Sabrina said.

"*Lieblings*, stay close to me," Granny said to the children.

The group approached the table tentatively, like they were sneaking up on a gorilla. Granny Relda was the first to take a seat, followed by Daphne, Robin Hood, and then Little John. Sabrina was happy to stand. She felt she could keep a better eye on the deranged Everafter if she were on her feet.

"It's a lovely party," Granny Relda said.

"Thank you," Red Riding Hood said as she gestured to an empty plate at the center of the table. "Would you care for a cookie? My grandmother made them."

"Thank you," the old woman replied. She reached over and pretended to take one of the imaginary cookies. Robin and Little John did the same, while Red Riding Hood poured imaginary tea from a pot into everyone's cups.

"Red, how are you feeling?" Granny asked.

"They took my basket," the little girl said. "I need my basket. I have to take it to my grandmother's house. She's very ill."

"I'm sure they will give it back to you, Red. We were wondering if we could ask you some questions," Robin said, then pretended to take a sip of his tea.

"I have questions," Red said. "So many questions. The people in the white coats won't answer them, though. They say it's all my imagination."

"Well, how about if we play a little game? You can ask me a question and I will try to answer it, and then I'll ask you a question and you can do the same," Granny Relda said.

"Games! I love games!" Red cried. "Me first!"

"Very well, what is your question?" Granny replied, as Robin Hood took a tape recorder from his briefcase and turned it on.

"Where is my kitty?" Red asked.

Granny looked at the girls for help. It was clear she didn't understand Red's question, but Sabrina knew all too well what Red wanted to know. She was referring to the Jabberwocky she had used to terrorize the town. It was a nearly unstoppable killing machine with a thousand teeth, but to Red it was a cuddly kitten. The family had used an enchanted sword known as the Vorpal blade to kill it.

"She's talking about the Jabberwocky," Sabrina whispered.

Granny's face flushed. "Red, your kitty is sleeping."

"Sleeping?"

"Yes, he went to sleep and he didn't wake up," Granny said.

"Oh," Red said, then grew quiet. "I love my kitty."

"Perhaps you could get a new one," Robin Hood said.

"A smaller one with less teeth," Sabrina replied.

"And one that doesn't breath fire," Daphne added.

"Your turn!" Red said, rebounding from her sadness.

"What can you tell us about the Wolf?" Robin asked.

Red Riding Hood peered at him for a long time. It was obvious that she was confused, but Sabrina remembered what Red had once called Mr. Canis.

"He means the doggie," Sabrina said. "You remember the doggie, right?"

"Oh, yes! The doggie," Red said. "I loved the doggie but he could be bad."

"Bad?"

"Very bad. He bit Grandma," Red said.

"We know," Granny Relda said. "We were wondering what you remember about the night he bit your grandma."

The little girl sat quietly for a moment. Her eyes drifted off as if she were struggling to remember something dancing on the edges of her mind. "Cages," she said softly, then looked around at the room. "So many cages."

Uncle Jake turned to Granny Relda. "What cages?"

Granny shook her head. "I've read nearly every version of the event and I've never seen any mention of cages."

"Red, can you tell us more about these cages?" Robin Hood asked.

"NO!" the child shrieked. There was so much anger and hate in her voice it startled even Little John. He nearly fell over his chair as he tried to back away.

"It was my turn to ask a question!" Red cried. "You have to play the game right."

"Of course, my friend," Granny said in a calming voice. "We didn't mean to skip your turn. What is your next question?"

"Can I go home?"

Sabrina shuddered. Her fear seemed to be shared. The rest of the group seemed just as unnerved by the suggestion. Ferryport Landing was on the verge of chaos already. The last thing it needed was Red walking around free. Eventually, Granny mustered the courage to answer. "You're very sick and you need to get better. Once that happens you can go home."

"I don't feel sick. I don't have a runny nose."

"That's because you are sick inside your mind. It's a different kind of illness. You can't feel it at all."

Red frowned. "OK."

"Can we ask a question, now?" Granny asked.

Red Riding Hood nodded.

"Tell us about these cages," Robin Hood said.

"The doggie was in one and then there was wind and then he wasn't in the cage anymore. The doggie wasn't in the doggie anymore. He was in the man. The man with the ax. He was an angry doggie. He made the other man scared. The other man cried. My turn! How is my baby brother?"

Granny searched the faces of the group for an answer but everyone was silent. She turned back to the child. "I didn't know you had a baby brother, Red."

"Oh yes," Red cooed. "He's got bright red hair, pink skin, and big green eyes. I just love him so much. Is someone taking care of him?"

Sabrina and Daphne looked at each other knowingly. They suspected that this baby brother of Red's wasn't really a relative, but a child she and the Jabberwocky had stolen. They had found a crib and baby toys in Red's hiding place, once, but who the child was or where he might be now was still a mystery.

"Yes," Granny lied. "He's perfectly safe."

"Good," Red sighed. "Your turn."

"You said that there was a man at your grandma's house," Robin Hood said. "Who was he?"

"Which one?"

Granny looked shocked. "I'm confused. Are you saying there were two men in your grandmother's house?"

Red nodded. "One was the doggie. One was the man."

"This is pointless," Sabrina whispered to her grandmother. "Even if she does remember what happened, she is so confused—how can we trust anything she says?"

Granny nodded reluctantly. "I'm afraid I agree. Perhaps we should go."

"Will you come and visit me again?" the little girl asked.

Sabrina cringed at the idea of making another visit to the murderous Everafter.

"We'll try," Granny said. "In the meantime you work on feeling better."

"Tell the doggie I said hello," Red said.

Once outside, Nurse Sprat set down her sandwich and went to work on the various locks and bolts that kept Red inside and safely away from others. Once Sabrina had calmed down, she noticed something in Robin and Little John's faces.

"What?" she asked.

"Something isn't adding up here," Robin said. "She spoke of cages. It might not mean anything, but I wouldn't be doing my job if I didn't look into it. I think we need to go see our furry friend again. I'm guessing there's a secret locked inside the cage in his head and we need to get it out."

• • •

Uncle Jake dropped the lawyers, his mother, the girls, and Barto off at the jailhouse, saying he needed to get back to the mirror and keep track of Goldilocks. Elvis also needed to be fed and let out of the house. Little John assured Jake he would keep the family safe. Barto was offended by this and claimed he didn't need the big man's help.

"Nottingham is never going to let us see Mr. Canis again," Daphne said.

Robin Hood smiled. "I think that's something my strong friend can remedy."

Little John grinned. "Finally! It's about time we started having some fun."

The big man walked over to a trash can, hefted it off the ground, and tossed it across the street and through the front window of a jewelry store. An alarm rang out that seemed to shake the air around Sabrina's ears.

"I suggest we hide," Robin said.

The family and their lawyers hurried around the corner of the jailhouse and ducked down behind some bushes. Seconds later, they watched Sheriff Nottingham rush out of the building and across the street. He glared at the broken window and then dashed inside the store.

"Let's go," Robin said.

The family raced inside the jailhouse and closed the door.

"John, I believe we might need the princess," Robin said.

Little John nodded. "I believe you're right. I'll bring her back as soon as I can, but you know how she gets. If there's a hair out of place she'll refuse to come."

"I'm sure you can persuade her," Robin replied.

The big man grinned. "My pleasure." Moments later, he was gone.

The group hurried back to the jail cells. Canis was slumped in the corner of his, breathing hard and attending to wounds he had suffered at the hands of the card soldiers. He looked tired, though Sabrina kept her distance. A tired Big Bad Wolf was still more dangerous than anything else known to man.

"Why have you come?" he said when he saw the family.

"We spoke to the child," Granny Relda said.

"You are wasting your time," Canis growled. "Can't you see your efforts are for nothing. Even if I wanted my freedom, Heart and Nottingham would never allow it."

"If we don't prove your innocence, they are going to put you to death," Robin said.

"So be it," Canis sniffed. "You cannot prove the innocence of a guilty man."

Everyone was quiet until Robin broke the silence. "Still, I believe we have a legitimate defense that needs to be explored. You and the Wolf are two separate beings sharing the same body. If that's true then we have to prove that you aren't in control when you are the Wolf. To do that we need to know exactly what happened that day."

Canis shook his head.

"C'mon, Mr. Canis," Daphne said. "You can at least answer some questions."

"Fine," Canis said. "What do you want to know?"

"What do you remember?" Robin asked.

Canis sat quietly for a long time, then sighed. "Nothing."

Granny Relda's face turned red and she angrily waved her finger at the old man. "Mr. Canis, you better start talking right now or I swear I'll . . . I'll . . . well, I don't know, but you won't like it!"

"Relda, I have no recollection of that day or any before it," Canis said. "When I am the Wolf I only see tiny moments, like snapshots of events. I remember the blood. I hear someone screaming but nothing is clear. When I am Canis I only know that something terrible has occurred."

"Red Riding Hood mentioned that she saw cages in her grandmother's house when she arrived that day. She says you were in one of them," Robin said.

Canis shook his head. "The child has an imagination. I wouldn't take what she says too seriously. The things the Wolf did that day . . . it was too much for a little girl to see. The damage I've done to that poor child's mind is inexcusable."

Just then, there was a terrific racket in the hallway. Sabrina gasped, fearing that Nottingham had returned, but when the door flew open she saw Little John, who was carrying a woman in a blue dress over his shoulder. The woman was holding a miniature pug in her hands. The little dog barked and snapped frantically.

"Here she is, boss," Little John said.

"John, you put me down this minute!" she cried. "I am royalty, you know. I have never been so offended in my life."

Robin approached the duo and looked up into the woman's face. "Hello, princess."

"Robin, so help me, if your lummox doesn't put me down this instant—"

"Of course," Robin chuckled. "You can set her down, John."

Little John eased the princess to her feet, and she complained bitterly about how he had wrinkled her expensive gown. When the woman was finished straightening her dress and looked up, Sabrina recognized her immediately. Her name was Beauty, though many people knew her because of her famous husband, the Beast. The duo were like night and day in appearance: She was a devastatingly attractive woman, he was a horrible nightmare with fur, yellow eyes, and tusks creeping out of his mouth. Sabrina had had a few run-ins with the couple already, and she knew the Beast was a member of the Scarlet Hand. Whether Beauty had joined as well, Sabrina didn't know.

"What are they doing here?" Beauty asked, alarmed.

"These are my clients," Robin said. "And they are in need of some of your special talents."

The little pug sniffed the air and yipped. The poor creature was wearing a little black doggie tuxedo, with a pocket square that matched his owner's dress and a tiny top hat. "Hush, Mr. Wuggles!" Beauty said, then turned her attention to the crowd. "Mr. Wuggles is not happy!" She proceeded to kiss the dog and speak to him in baby talk for several minutes.

"Boss, I don't think we've got a lot of time," Little John said. "Nottingham will be back when he gets bored."

"Good point," Robin said, and turned to Beauty. "Princess, we need you to hypnotize someone so we can ask some questions."

Beauty craned her neck to see into the cell. Her eyes grew wide and she shook her head. "Robin Hood, you've lost your mind if you think—"

"You're the only hope we have," Robin said.

"But that's the—"

"We know, but your husband was just as wild as the Wolf when you met him. You know the kind of effect you have on savages. If I thought we could get the information any other way, I would."

Beauty stepped up to the cell and looked inside. Mr. Wuggles did the same and whined. "Oh, boy," the princess sighed.

"What's she going to do?" Sabrina asked.

Beauty turned to her. "I calm down animals, even put them into hypnotic states. I guess you could say I'm the monster whisperer." Beauty turned back to the cage. "OK, pal. I'm going to come in there, but you have to promise not to eat me."

Canis nodded.

Little John raced to the cell door with a set of keys. "Nottingham ran out of here without them."

The cell door swung open. Beauty shoved her dog into Sabrina's arms and stepped inside. "Close the door," she said.

"And lock it," Canis added.

Little John did as he was told.

Beauty sat down on a crude chair next to Canis. "Well, are you ready to get started?"

Canis looked to Granny Relda with an expression of doubt.

"For me, old friend," Granny said.

Canis nodded.

Beauty rested her hand on Canis's muscular arm. All at once the tension in the old man seemed to dissolve. His body relaxed, and the wild animal scent that filled the room disappeared. The anger and hate in Canis's eyes were replaced with a calm, almost sleepy expression.

"Feel better?" the princess asked.

Canis nodded.

"What do you want to know?" Beauty asked the lawyers.

"Ask him to describe what happened the night Red Riding Hood's grandmother died," Robin replied.

"Awww, that's going to be so gross," Beauty complained. She pointed at Sabrina. "You, cover Mr. Wuggles's ears. He's very sensitive. I don't want him hearing this."

Sabrina did her best, though the dog refused to cooperate. Instead, he squirmed in Sabrina's arms until he was facing her, then proceeded to lick every inch of her face.

"OK, big guy," Beauty said to Canis. "I want you to hear my voice only. You will see only what I ask you to see and though what you might see will be shocking, it won't bother you at all. In fact, it will be like you are watching a movie."

"OK," Canis said and he closed his eyes.

"Let's go back in time. I want you to go back to one night in particular. It was the night you met Little Red Riding Hood. Are you there?"

"Yes."

"Good. Tell me what you see and hear."

Canis shook his head. "It's fuzzy. I can't make out anything."

"Concentrate," Beauty said. "Try to bring it into focus."

Canis's body went into convulsions. His head swung back and forth violently.

"He's fighting me," Beauty told the crowd.

"Keep trying," Little John replied as he nervously watched the door for Nottingham's return.

"It doesn't work like that," Beauty snapped. "It's not a matter of trying harder. His brain opens up or it doesn't. There's something he doesn't want to tell me."

Suddenly, Canis relaxed. "I'm running."

"Where to?" Beauty asked.

"There's a tiny house in the woods."

"Do you see anything else?" Beauty asked.

"Light is blinding me and the trees are leaning over," he said.

"He's talking crazy like Red," Sabrina whispered to her grandmother.

"Why are the trees leaning over?" Beauty asked, ignoring Sabrina's comment.

Canis shook his head. "The wind is incredible. I'm pounding on the door. I want him to follow me, but he's afraid."

"Who is afraid?" Beauty repeated.

Canis was silent. "I can't see him anymore. I'm inside the house. The old woman is there. The child is crying."

"Are you talking about Red Riding Hood?" Beauty asked.

Canis nodded. "Then there is wind. So much wind."

Beauty turned to the lawyers. "Is any of this making sense to you?"

Robin shrugged. "Ask him if he sees any cages."

Beauty repeated the question, and for a long moment the old man was silent. Then he nodded.

"Yes, cages," he said. "Something is in one of them, but the wind is so strong I can't see it. It's some kind of animal. It's out! It's coming at me!" Canis let out a horrible scream that startled everyone, then his eyes flickered open and he looked at Beauty. "Who's that playing around in my head?" he growled.

The princess fell backward and ran toward the cage door. Luckily, the chains that bound the Wolf's arms and legs held him back. He laughed at her fear and promised he would kill her someday. Then he looked over at the Grimm family and smiled. "Your day is coming, too."

Once Little John helped Beauty out of the cell, Canis seemed to regain control of himself. He apologized and slumped back into his corner while the big lawyer locked the cell door tight.

"I've lost the connection," Beauty said, as she caught her breath. "Not even my soon-to-be ex-husband was this difficult."

"You and Beast are splitting up?" Robin said with a sly grin.

"Does your wife, Marian, know what kind of a flirt you are?" Beauty said with a little laugh.

Sabrina's heart sank. Robin was married.

"Beauty, the two of you have been together for centuries," Granny said.

"He's in the Scarlet Hand. I can't convince him to give it up, and I just can't reach him anymore. He's not the man I married."

"So you haven't joined?" Daphne asked.

"No, I'm no revolutionary," Beauty said. "I remember the last time this nonsense came up. That's how we all got stuck in this town. Beast says Everafters should be in charge. He says the Master is going to rule the world, and we'll enslave the human race, blah, blah, blah . . . I'll have none of it. All I want from this world is a new pair of shoes every day for the rest of my life."

She reached over to Sabrina and took her dog. "And of course a diamond-studded collar for Mr. Wuggles," she cooed to the dog. She showered the slobbery little mutt with kisses and he licked her face happily.

"The only thing you're going to get is the edge of my blade, you traitorous idiot," a voice bellowed from the doorway. The group spun around to see Nottingham step into the room, his curved dagger clenched firmly in his hand.

6

ottingham charged at Beauty but Little John punched him in the face, knocking him backward against the bars of a jail cell. The sheriff groaned but lunged again, and soon Sabrina and Daphne were caught in the middle of a melee of flying fists and slashing daggers. Sabrina snatched her sister by the arm and fought her way out of the chaos until they joined their grandmother, Barto, Beauty, and Mr. Wuggles huddled in a corner. Soon, the lawyers had managed to subdue the evil sheriff. They had him flat on his back, while he kicked and cursed at them. Sabrina rushed over to help, grabbing Nottingham's flailing leg and holding it down.

"You're all going to join your mongrel friend at the end of a hangman's noose," Nottingham seethed, his deadly dagger still several feet from his greedy fingers.

"What are we going to do with him?" Beauty asked. "He'll tell everyone I was helping you. You don't want to be on the wrong side of the Scarlet Hand these days, even if your husband is a member."

"Princess, have you ever done your little hypnotizing trick on a person?" Robin asked Beauty.

"Never tried," she said. "I think it only works on beasts."

"Well, he's about as beastly as a man can get," Little John said.

Beauty reached down and placed her hand on Nottingham's forehead. He fought a moment longer but then relaxed. "Go to sleep," she said, and a moment later the sheriff was out cold. "Sheriff, you're not going to remember the fight that just happened. You aren't going to remember that you found us in the jail. You aren't going to remember me or anyone who was here."

"I won't?" the sheriff asked, dreamily.

"No, you won't."

"OK."

Robin Hood cleared his throat. "I saw a hypnotist plant a secret message in a person once. You know, every time he heard a certain word the man would cluck like a chicken. Could we get Nottingham to do something like that, I mean, while we have him hypnotized?"

Little John grinned. "You're a genius."

Beauty laughed. "What do you think, Mr. Wuggles?"

The dog barked.

"Mr. Wuggles thinks that's an excellent idea."

• • •

It had been a long day. When Sabrina finally plopped down on the sofa and kicked off her shoes, she found blisters on the backs of her heels. Daphne was almost asleep on her feet, and Granny Relda, who usually had more energy than both the girls combined, fell into a chair and propped her legs up on an ottoman. Elvis trotted down the stairs and went from one person to the next, delivering kisses.

Uncle Jake came down to tell the girls that his search for Goldilocks was on hold. She had hopped a flight out of Venice following the incident in the canal, and he had been unable to figure out exactly where she was going. They would have to wait until she landed to proceed. Sabrina was a little disappointed. Tracking down their elusive heroine might have been a nice distraction from the image that kept appearing in her mind. The Wolf was inside her head.

Even as she lay in bed that night she couldn't stop seeing his monstrous face, promising that he was going to kill her and her family as soon as he got the chance. She remembered his smiling eyes. It gave him pleasure to terrify her, and he had succeeded. She wanted to talk about it with someone, anyone, but when she had mentioned Mr. Canis's lack of control to the rest of the family she had been punished. No one wanted to see him for what he was.

Sabrina turned to her sister. Daphne was sound asleep, as if the Wolf's threats meant nothing. She was so trusting—so naïve. Like the rest of her family, she was tucked in her bed, never thinking that death might crawl out of the closet and gobble her whole. There would be nothing Sabrina could do to stop it, either, not as long as her sister refused to retrieve the secret weapon the three pigs swore could save them all. Why had Hamstead entrusted such a huge responsibility to such a little girl? Daphne was too young for such a heavy burden. Sure, Daphne had a knack with enchanted items, and Sabrina—well, Sabrina and magic didn't mix, but whatever was in that safe-deposit box had to be used by someone who saw things clearly. Someone who put sentimentality aside and fought for her family. That key could stop the Wolf, maybe even put Mr. Canis back in control. Either way, the danger would be over. If the family had this weapon things might even get easier for them in the town. They could fight the Scarlet Hand. With such a weapon, the evil group's threats would be meaningless. There were lots of reasons to have the weapon. It was time to go get it, even if Daphne didn't think so. Sabrina knew what had to be done.

She leaned over and gently unfastened the chain from her sister's neck. The little girl was such a sound sleeper, she didn't seem to notice it was gone. Sabrina held up the key and studied it, imagining the possibilities. Then she crawled out of bed, pulled on a pair of jeans, a black shirt, and sneakers and padded down the hallway to Mirror's room. Once inside, Mirror's horrifying face immediately appeared, accompanied by frightening bolts of lightning and a wall of flames that streaked across her path.

"Who dares invade my sanctuary!" Mirror bellowed.

"Turn off the special effects," Sabrina said. "It's me!"

The threatening image faded and the fire snuffed out, replaced by the kind face of her friend. "Up a little late, aren't you, Starfish?"

"I'm on a secret mission," Sabrina replied.

"Is this mission secret from your grandmother?"

Sabrina nodded, then turned her attention to the traveler's chest. She recited the address to the bank and bent over to lift the lid but it was locked tight. Uncle Jake must have taken the key. She'd have to use plan B to get to the bank, even if it nauseated her. "I need the flying carpet."

"What for?"

"I can't tell you," she said.

"No surprise, there. Still, where's your sister? Where's Puck? You never go alone."

"This time I have to," Sabrina said, holding out her set of keys to the Hall of Wonders.

"I don't know about this, kiddo," Mirror said.

"I won't be gone long. Trust me. I'm doing this for everyone's good," Sabrina said as she opened the spare room's one and only window.

Mirror's hand broke the surface of the reflection and took the keys. "I swear, you're giving me gray hair," he said as he faded away. Moments later he returned with Sabrina's keys and Aladdin's carpet. "Would you listen if I asked you to be careful?"

Sabrina nodded as she opened the window. "I always listen."

"Yes, but do you hear me?"

She unrolled the rug on the floor, admiring the beautifully embroidered designs of the stars, moons, and sabers. Then she sat down in the center and clenched its tassels in her hands. "OK, rug, take me to the Ferryport Landing Savings and Loan."

"What's at the bank?" Mirror asked.

"The answer to a lot of our problems," Sabrina replied.

Moments later, the rug was darting toward downtown, the air whipping Sabrina's hair behind her as she soared over the treetops. She concentrated on the weapon she would soon possess. Whatever it was, Swineheart and Boarman said it was powerful. If it helped three out-of-shape piggies beat a monster, it might just be what her family needed. She clutched Daphne's little key in her hand and imagined what might be inside the safe-deposit box. Perhaps it was a bazooka, or a laser gun, or some kind of device that fired lava.

Soon the bank came into sight and the little rug floated to the ground. It landed on the deserted sidewalk in front of the building. Sabrina glanced around, careful that no one was watching as she stepped off the carpet. It automatically rolled itself up and Sabrina stashed it behind a nearby bush.

The streetlights that once illuminated the quaint neighborhood were black and burned out. Ferryport Landing's Main Street had never been Broadway, but now it seemed desperately lonely. With the coast clear, she climbed the steps of the bank. Before she tried the door she noticed a sign that read CLOSED. Sabrina could have kicked herself. Of course the bank was going to be closed. It was nighttime. Her over-eagerness to retrieve the weapon kept her from thinking clearly. Now what was she going to do? She couldn't go back home and try during the day. Her family was always around and Daphne would notice that the key was missing.

She sat down on the stoop, contemplating her limited choices, when a crazy thought popped into her head. Why not break into the bank? She had done lots of crazy things since moving to Ferryport Landing. Why would this one be any crazier? She could break a window and crawl inside. If she hurried, she could open the safe-deposit box, grab the weapon, and escape before Nottingham arrived. It was as good a plan as any.

She stood up and studied the bank, sizing it up like it was an adversary. She had broken out of many places in her lifetime. As foster children, she and her sister were constantly escaping the lunatics the state sent them to live with. She recalled the Deasy family, who owned and operated an ostrich farm in Hoboken, New Jersey. The birds were mean and frightening, chasing Daphne nearly nonstop for the first three days. When one of them spit in Sabrina's face, she knew that the sisters Grimm had to go. After a week of trying, Sabrina managed to pick the lock on the front gate, freeing herself and Daphne and the entire herd of stinky giant birds. She and her sister hopped the gate on the underground train that led to New York City, and they were back in the Big Apple hours before the Hoboken Police Department managed to track and capture the first of the Deasys' twenty-five ostriches. If Sabrina could pick a lock, she could certainly throw a rock through a window.

Sabrina searched the street for a stone heavy enough to crack the bank's thick security windows. She found a good sharp one and headed back to spot a place to fling it. She circled around the back of the building, found a window low to the ground, and peeked inside. There were wires attached to the window that led to a bright red bell on the wall. She guessed the bell would start to wail if the windows were broken. Once she was inside, she'd have to act fast. The last thing she needed was for Nottingham to show up and decide to be a police officer for once. She closed her eyes and said a silent prayer, then reared back, aimed, and tossed the rock. She prepared for the shattering of glass but it never came. Instead she heard a voice.

"Sabrina Grimm turns to a life of crime. I'm so proud of you."

Sabrina recognized the voice immediately. It was Puck, and he had her rock clenched firmly in his hand.

"What are you doing here?" Sabrina demanded, dragging him into the shadows.

"Keeping an eye on you," Puck said. "You slipped past all my security."

"I'm not going to stay locked up in the house just 'cause you say we should," Sabrina said. "I can take care of myself."

"You are truly an ungrateful jerk. Do you know how much money I have to pay the troglodyte to sit inside the dirty clothes hamper? Not to mention the brownies living in the bushes outside and the ogre under the couch. Professionals are not cheap. Plus, I have to pay their dental insurance and contribute to their 401(k) plans. But do you appreciate it? NO! You run around this town willy-nilly, as if you had a death wish. Well, listen, bub, if your family gets killed, then I'm out in the cold. That means no more free meals. No more cable TV. Do you know what would happen to me if I had to go back down to just three or four channels?" Puck shuddered.

"Listen, everyone appreciates what you're trying to do," Sabrina said. "But at the moment, it's getting in my way. Now, hand over that rock. I need it."

"Hey, you don't have to tell me about the need to break things," Puck said. "If I don't smash a window four or five times a day I don't feel like myself. Still, it doesn't seem like your style."

"I'm not breaking windows just to break something. I need to get into the bank. There's something inside I have to get," Sabrina said.

"That's what all the bank robbers say."

"I'm not robbing the bank!"

"Then what are you going to steal? They chain the pens to the counters, you know."

"I'm not stealing anything. I'm breaking in to get something that was given to me, and I can't wait for the bank to open."

"But you plan on breaking something to do it, right?"

"Yes."

"OK, I'll help."

Sabrina felt like telling Puck to get lost, but she realized the fairy boy had some skills that might come in handy. Puck could do all kinds of things that human beings couldn't.

"Actually—" Sabrina said.

Puck grinned and tossed the rock aside. "Allow me to call some friends." He took a small wooden flute from his pocket and blasted a few notes into it. Moments later, they were standing in a tornado of little lights. There were hundreds of them buzzing past Sabrina's face, clicking and chirping. Puck raised his hands and all the lights stopped in midair. Sabrina had met these creatures before. They were pixies, and they obeyed every command Puck gave them.

"Minions," he said, "we need to get into this bank."

The group of lights squeaked and flew toward the bank's window. They seemed to study it for a moment, then they flew off, circling the building as if looking for a crack or crevice to invade. Moments later, Sabrina saw a few of them flying around inside the bank. They hovered in the window and buzzed to Puck.

"They're opening the door for us now," Puck said. Sabrina and Puck rushed around to the front door and hurried inside. Sabrina closed the door behind them in case anyone strolling down the street noticed it was wide open.

"I believe the words you're looking for are 'thank you,'" Puck said.

Sabrina rolled her eyes. "We've got to act fast. This place might have a silent alarm, and if that's the case, Nottingham is probably on his way."

"What are we looking for?"

"Safe-deposit boxes. You'll find them in a room with little drawers built into the walls."

Puck repeated the description to the pixies and they flew off in different directions. Sabrina went searching on her own, opening one door after another. Each room she searched was a dead end, and each dead end made her more and more aware that Nottingham could arrive at any moment.

Luckily, Puck called out that the room had been found. She raced back the way she came and found him hovering in a doorway at the opposite end of the building. In the room they found three walls, each lined with little silver doors. The fourth wall supported an enormous round door that protected the valuables in the bank's vault. Sabrina studied one drawer carefully. It had a number carved into its door and a tiny lock. Sabrina reached into her pocket and removed the silver key. The number printed on it read TH192.

"I need to open TH192," she said, scanning the wall. There were so many doors. It could take hours to find the right one.

"What's the big deal about this safe-deposit box?" Puck asked as he joined the search. Sabrina knew she couldn't keep her secret from him any longer.

"Before we left New York City, Sheriff Hamstead gave Daphne this key and told her it opened a box that contained a powerful weapon. He told her to get it if Mr. Canis ever lost control of the Wolf. Hamstead said it was the only thing that could truly stop him."

"If he gave it to Daphne, then how come you have it?" Puck asked.

Sabrina felt her face go red. "She doesn't understand."

"You stole it?"

Sabrina nodded. "I had to."

Puck looked surprised.

"What? Are you disappointed? Is the Trickster King going to give me a lecture on being a good person? I'm doing this for the good of us all," Sabrina argued. "This weapon might be able to fix Mr. Canis, too, and fight the Scarlet Hand. Then you could let your security guards go."

Puck said nothing; he didn't have to. Sabrina could sense his disapproval, though it boggled the mind. Who was Puck to tell her how to behave?

"Here it is," he said.

Sabrina rushed to his side and checked the number on the

drawer—it matched the one on the silver key. She slipped the key into the slot, turned it, and felt the latch open. Inside was a long metal box with a handle. She pulled it out, her mind swirling with possibilities. Carefully, she opened the top of the box. Inside was a small blue velvet bag tied at the top with string. The words THE NORTH WIND were stitched on the fabric in gold. Sabrina took the bag in her hand. Whatever was inside was small and cylindrical. She was surprised by how light it was.

Sabrina untied the string and opened the bag. Wary of touching a magical item, she peered into the sack. She expected to find an ancient amulet that could shoot electricity or perhaps a magic wand, but instead, much to her surprise, she found a kazoo.

"What is it?" Puck said. He pulled the kazoo from the sack and examined it closely. "This is your secret weapon?"

Sabrina was too crushed to speak. She felt as if someone had just punched her in the stomach. All of her hopes, all of her needs, and all of her plans had just vanished before her eyes, replaced by someone's idea of a twisted joke. "It's a toy," Sabrina said. "It's a child's toy."

"How is this going to stop the Big Bad Wolf?"

"It won't, you idiot. It's a kazoo. Can't you see? It's someone's idea of a prank." She stormed out of the room and out the front

door of the bank. Somehow that triggered the alarm and an ear-splitting bell started ringing.

"Hey! You can't just walk away on your own," Puck said, chasing after her. "You need protection."

"Why?" Sabrina said as she stepped out into the street. "What does it matter? The whole town is trying to kill us. My grandmother's best friend is a murderer. We're all dead anyway."

"You still have me," Puck said.

Sabrina scowled but said nothing.

"You don't think I can protect you, do you?" Puck asked.

"I don't think anyone can, Puck," Sabrina cried. "At least not now."

Puck's face flushed red, but he said nothing.

"C'mon, we better get back to the house," Sabrina said, changing her tone. She knew she had hurt him, but did he really expect that she would put her family's safety in the hands of an immature fairy whose biggest enemy was a bar of soap?

"Just a minute," Puck said as he stared at the little toy flute. "Maybe there's something more to this kazoo. How does it work?"

"It's a toy, Puck," she said, snatching it out of his hands. "You blow into it."

She put the kazoo into her mouth, took a deep breath, and

blew. She had used a kazoo before. She knew there was a trick to making the sound—a sort of hum/blow into one end that makes a fuzzy musical note come out the other. But this kazoo didn't do that. Instead, she felt the familiar uncomfortable tingle of magic. Then there was a horrible *whooshing* sound and an intense whipping wind and right before her eyes the windows of the bank imploded. The roof flew off the building and the walls crumbled. Even the paint on the sign peeled off and blew away, along with every nail, screw, and two-by-four. In a matter of seconds there was no evidence that a bank or any other kind of building had ever stood in front of her. When the wind died down, all that was left of the bank was the alarm, ringing loudly as if there was still something to protect.

Sabrina gaped at the kazoo, speechless.

"Well, if you don't want it, I'll take it," Puck said.

7

abrina and Puck slipped back into the house without incident. After returning the flying carpet to Mirror, Puck followed Sabrina into her bedroom. There they found Daphne, still solidly asleep and producing deep, loud snores that sounded like a lovesick moose. Sabrina carefully placed the necklace and safe-deposit box key back around the little girl's neck and breathed a sigh of relief that she hadn't been caught. Puck watched from the corner with a frown on his face.

"Don't give me any grief. I did what had to be done," Sabrina said as she kicked off her shoes. She was too tired to put her pajamas back on and instead crawled under the blankets fully dressed.

"No lecture," Puck said. "Still, we need to get something clear. From now on you need to check in with your bodyguards before you sneak out."

"I can't sneak out if someone knows I'm sneaking out," Sabrina argued. "That takes the sneakiness out of the sneak. Besides, you're taking this whole security thing too far. I don't need bodyguards. I can handle myself just fine, and now that we have the kazoo . . ."

"So you're not going to cooperate?"

Sabrina shook her head, sleepily. "No, I'm not and there's nothing you can do about it."

Puck grinned. "Then I suppose I'm just helpless then, huh? I guess you've won?"

"Now you're getting it," Sabrina said. "Now go back to bed. I'm tired."

Sabrina braced herself for another argument, but much to her surprise Puck turned and left the room.

Sabrina smiled and nestled into her bed. *I think that boy is finally getting some sense*, she thought. As she drifted off to sleep, she reached into her pants pocket and removed the sack that held the kazoo. She could feel the unhealthy ache that magic produced, but the bag seemed to dull the sensation. Regardless, she would have to be careful. Maybe she should find a hiding place for it so that the temptation didn't overtake her. She had to be strong this time. After all, she couldn't count on the others. This time, she was on her own.

• • •

The next morning, Sabrina awoke to a blinding light. The rising sun was flooding through her bedroom window and right into her eyes. She would have to remember to pull the blinds in the future. She reached for a pillow to pull over her head, but her wrist was caught on something. She sat up in bed and held her left hand up to her face. There was a steel bracelet wrapped tightly around her wrist. It was connected to a strong chain that was linked to a similar bracelet that was attached to the wrist of a shaggy-haired boy who was sleeping in a rocking chair next to her bed.

"PUCK!" Sabrina cried, pulling so hard on her end of the handcuffs that the boy fairy tumbled out of the chair and onto the floor. Unfortunately, the fall dragged her out of bed as well and she fell on top of him.

"What's the story, morning glory?" Puck said, rubbing the sleep from his eyes.

"What is this about?" Sabrina said, raising her hand and shaking the handcuff, thus shaking Puck's arm as well.

"Unfortunately, it's necessary," Puck explained. "You don't want to work with my security staff, so from now on I'm going to be your personal bodyguard. I'm going to be with you every second of the day."

"This is insanity," Sabrina said as she tried in vain to free herself.

"Trust me, being downwind of you twenty-four hours a day is not what I call a good time, but you've left me no choice."

Sabrina screamed. "Give me the key!"

Puck reached into his pocket and took out a tiny golden key. "Is this what you want?"

"Give it to me, pus face!"

"Are you going to work with your bodyguards?"

"Forget it. You're not going to blackmail me," Sabrina said.

And at that, Puck put the key into his mouth and swallowed it. Sabrina screamed again.

"Are you deranged?" she yelled as she climbed to her feet, dragging Puck up as she went. Sabrina marched toward the door but was held back by the boy. She turned and saw that he was enjoying the tug of war, so she pulled hard and dragged him out into the hallway in search of her grandmother.

Granny Relda was not supportive of Sabrina's crisis. In fact, she, Uncle Jake, and Daphne found the whole situation hilarious. They snickered all through breakfast. "Sabrina, Puck is just trying to be helpful," Granny said. "Perhaps you do need a little personal attention, and there's not much I can do about it anyway. If he swallowed the key, all we can do is wait."

"Wait for what?" Sabrina asked, then suddenly realized what they would be waiting for and had to fight to keep her breakfast down.

"I wouldn't hold your breath on that one," Puck said as he reached his hand into a bowl of oatmeal and shoveled it into his mouth. Sabrina's hand was dragged along and covered with the gooey cereal.

"How am I going to get dressed? Or take a bath?" Sabrina cried.

"Who needs a bath?" Puck said, wiping the extra oatmeal on his shirt.

"I suppose we could just take the two of you out in the yard and hose you down," Uncle Jake said.

"Elvis loves it," Daphne said.

Uncle Jake laughed so hard his scrambled eggs fell out of his mouth.

Daphne finished her breakfast, and for the first time ever, Sabrina watched the little girl push her empty plate away. There was no such word as *full* in her sister's vocabulary. Since the girl had more of Sabrina's clothes on, as well as high-heel shoes, she guessed that Daphne was still a "grown-up." "I had a thought last night," Daphne offered.

"Oh?" Granny said.

"There's one eyewitness we haven't talked to," Daphne said. "The woodcutter."

Granny's eyes lit up. "*Liebling*, that's good detective work. I totally forgot there was someone else at the grandmother's house."

"So, do you know where he lives?" Uncle Jake asked.

Granny shrugged. "I'm afraid I don't. There are thousands of Everafters in this town and I haven't met them all. There's also a chance that he doesn't live here. As you know, some of the Everafters moved away before Wilhelm's barrier went up, and others never came to America at all."

"How can we find out?" Daphne asked.

Granny clapped her hands, jumped from her seat, and rushed to the family journals. "We need to get back to our research. Perhaps he does live here in Ferryport Landing. He could be a great help to our case."

"I'll help," Sabrina said eagerly.

Granny cocked an eyebrow, obviously surprised by Sabrina's enthusiasm. "You will?"

Sabrina nodded, though she didn't feel entirely honest. The thought of freeing Mr. Canis terrified her, but she wanted to get back into the family's good graces, especially her grandmother's.

"Thank you, *liebling*," Granny said.

Sabrina dragged Puck from his chair and pulled him into the living room, where she snatched a copy of the complete fairy tales of Charles Perrault. She dragged him back to the table and sat down. According to the copyright, Perrault was one of the first people to document the ghastly tale of Red Riding Hood.

His book was published in 1697, and his account described a woodcutter who came to Red Riding Hood's rescue. Sabrina was impressed with the man's heroics. Not too many people had gone face-to-face with the Wolf and lived to tell the tale. Sabrina noted the story and continued her research.

All the Grimms who had lived in Ferryport Landing had kept detailed journals of their adventures. Even Sabrina and Daphne had filled a couple. It was the family responsibility to document anything unusual that occurred in the Everafter community. With this sizable collection at their fingertips, it was obvious to everyone that there were a lot of unusual occurrences in the sleepy river town. Sabrina scanned hundreds of entries. She read about a short-lived military overthrow of the mouse king of Oz. She found sheet music composed by a jazz trumpeter named Boy Blue. She even learned that the Three Blind Mice had once applied for seeing-eye dogs. Generations of Grimms had collected these stories, but Sabrina didn't find anything else on the woodcutter or what had become of him.

She closed the last of her share of the journals and sat back in her chair. "I've got nothing."

Granny sighed. "I didn't find anything, either."

Daphne looked up from her book. "What does the word *mani . . . mani . . . fest* mean?"

"You mean *manifest*. It's a list of items that are shipped on a train, bus, truck, whatever," Granny explained.

"Where's your dictionary?" Sabrina asked.

Daphne stuck her tongue out and turned her attention back to Granny Relda. "Can it be a list of people, too?"

"Sure," the old woman said. "What did you find?"

"This. It looks like a list of the passengers on Wilhelm's boat," the little girl said, handing several sheets of paper to her grandmother.

Granny took the papers. "Good work, Daphne. I should have thought of this. Let's see if there's a woodcutter on this list." Granny perused the list. "Hmm, I'm not seeing anyone."

Sabrina reached over and took the list from her grandmother. Sure enough, there was no "woodcutter" on the list. "If only we knew what his name is," she said.

"Well, we don't need that. We know everyone else's name. Let's go through the list and find the people we've never heard of," Granny said. "Assuming that he got on Wilhelm's boat."

Puck wasn't thrilled. "Is this going to take long? I have plans."

"The handcuffs were your idea, buster. Any chance we're going to see that key pop up?" Sabrina said.

Puck shook his head.

The Grimms went through the list, checking off everyone they knew by name. There were quite a number of people in Ferryport Landing who just had titles for names: the Mad Hatter, the Beast, the Sheriff of Nottingham, or the Queen of Hearts, for example. That made the search much easier. Soon, there was a list of only twenty citizens neither Granny, Sabrina, nor Daphne could identify. Seven of them had odd, almost unpronounceable names, and Granny guessed they were either witches, goblins, or trolls. Eight more were names that were obviously for animals, including Hans the Hedgehog and someone called the Sawhorse. That left five names, and two of them were women.

Just then, the phone rang. Granny answered it and cried out in excitement when she heard the caller's voice. "Little John! We've been trying to track down another eyewitness. We believe the woodcutter might actually live in Ferryport Landing. What's that? Oh, of course. We'll be right there."

Granny hung up the phone.

"What's going on?" Uncle Jake asked.

"Bluebeard has a new witness and they're starting the trial early today. We have to go over there now!"

"Who's the witness?" Daphne asked.

"His name is Howard Hatchett," Granny replied.

Sabrina sighed. "He's on our list. Howard Hatchett is the woodcutter."

• • •

The group drove up and down Main Street looking for a parking space. Granny commented that she had never seen the downtown area so busy, even when there were other humans living in town. While they searched, they passed the site where the bank had once stood.

"I've heard of people robbing banks, but I've never heard of anyone stealing the bank itself," Uncle Jake said as Granny peered out her window at the vacant lot.

"That's quite peculiar," Granny said. "Unfortunately, it's a mystery that's going to have to wait."

Daphne poked her head out the window and craned her neck for a better view. When she pulled herself back inside the car she looked panicked and nervous. She turned to Sabrina and mouthed the words, "What happened?"

Sabrina shrugged, though her heart burned for the betrayal she was committing. Sabrina knew what was going on in her sister's mind. Daphne believed the weapon was lost. Sabrina knew she should tell, and from the look on Puck's face, he agreed, but she wasn't sure how to explain. When Daphne reached up to touch the necklace, Sabrina could almost hear the remorse running through her sister's mind.

Uncle Jake finally parked the car and the family trudged up the steps toward the courtroom. Once inside, Daphne yanked on Sabrina's sleeve and told Granny they would meet them inside in a moment. Granny agreed but told the children not to dillydally. Mr. Canis needed their support.

"OK, I was wrong," said Daphne as she leaned against a wall. The little girl looked like she needed it to prevent herself from collapsing. Her face was red and tears were swimming in her eyes. "We should have gotten the weapon while we could. Now, we'll never get it. You saw the bank. It's gone."

Sabrina nodded but said nothing.

"I should have listened to you," the little girl continued.

"Yes, well, it's too late for that," Sabrina said. "You wanted to be in charge and—"

Puck kicked her in the leg and gave her an angry look.

"What are we going to do about the weapon?" Daphne cried. "What if we didn't go get it 'cause I was being stubborn and it turns out we need it?"

Puck glared at Sabrina. "I have a feeling it will turn up."

The courtroom door opened and Granny poked her head out. "Come along, *lieblings*. The trial is staring."

The courtroom was standing room only and curious citizens

were spilling out into the hall. News of the trial had obviously spread, and Everafters from all over town had come to see what everyone was referring to as "the trial of every century."

Mayor Heart and Sheriff Nottingham gazed at the capacity crowd with delight. Sabrina overheard Heart suggesting that they should have sold tickets. Nottingham agreed and they both broke into laughter.

Several of the family's friends came over to offer their support. Gepetto had closed his toy store to come and be by the family's side. Cinderella and her human husband, Tom, came over and offered to bring the family dinner, though Granny declined. Mr. Seven sat on a stack of phonebooks in the back row and even Briar Rose's fairy godmothers wished the family well, while staring daggers at Uncle Jake. But most surprising was Snow White, who eased into their row and sat down next to Granny Relda. She said nothing, just took the old woman's hand in her own and held it.

"I'm sorry, Snow," the old woman said.

"I know you would never do anything to hurt me on purpose, Relda. I'm sorry, too," Ms. White replied.

Briar Rose joined the group. She sat down next to Uncle Jake and took his hand. Uncle Jake smiled. "You sure you want the whole town knowing you're dating a Grimm?"

Briar nodded and kissed him on the cheek. There was a light

in the couple's eyes and laughter in their voices. Sabrina had seen the same expressions on her parents' faces every day that she could remember. The sleepy princess and her swashbuckling uncle were in love.

Robin Hood and Little John entered the courtroom just as several card soldiers led Mr. Canis to his table. Robin patted him on the shoulder, then opened his briefcase. He rifled through some papers and watched Bluebeard out of the corner of his eye. Bluebeard stopped at the Grimms' row and bent in close to smile at Ms. White.

"Snow, someone should arrest you. It has to be a crime to be so beautiful," he said.

Snow gave a forced smile, but when the creepy man turned away, Sabrina caught her rolling her eyes in disgust. Sabrina looked over and spotted her little sister doing the same.

"All rise!" the Three of Spades shouted. "The honorable Judge Hatter is now presiding."

Judge Hatter marched through a side door. He was carrying a sledgehammer on his shoulder and tripping over his long black robes. When he got to his seat, he set the sledgehammer down and looked around the courtroom.

"Oh, you're back. Well, I suppose we should start the trial," he said. He picked up his sledgehammer and slammed it down on the desk, practically destroying it. "Mr. Bluebeard, do you have another witness?"

"Indeed I do! The prosecution calls Howard Hatchett."

The double doors at the back of the room opened and a man in a flashy blue suit entered. He had a bushy red beard and a veiny nose. He was wearing a bright red ball cap with a logo advertising something called Hatchettland. He looked nervous, especially when he saw Mr. Canis. He even tried to run away several times, but two card soldiers stopped him and forced him into the witness stand.

Hatchett sat down, but he never took his eyes off Canis. Even when Bluebeard approached him and thanked him for taking the time to testify, Hatchett didn't seem to hear him.

"Mr. Hatchett, are you well?" Bluebeard asked.

"I'm fine," Hatchett said, shifting in his seat. "I have to admit I never thought I'd see this day."

"Mr. Hatchett, could you tell the jury who you are and how you are related to this case," Bluebeard asked.

Hatchett stammered. "My name is Howard Hatchett. Some people know me as the woodcutter or the hunter from the story of Red Riding Hood."

Sabrina watched Canis frown.

"And you were there the day of the incident?"

Hatchett nodded, keeping his eyes on Canis.

"What kind of work are you in, Mr. Hatchett?"

"Well, I . . . I used to be a woodcutter. I cut down trees and sold the lumber to mills. I started out working for a man but then I saw an opportunity and went into business for myself." Hatchett sat quietly, watching Canis. After a few minutes, his expression changed from fear to confusion, and he continued. "Then one day I thought to myself, 'Hey! I'm one of literature's greatest heroes.'"

"What did he say?" Daphne whispered.

"He's bragging," Puck replied.

"I saved Little Red Riding Hood's life. I'm an idol to millions. I faced the Big Bad Wolf and lived to tell about it. I'm famous and beloved. So I started a company to provide products to people who want to be more like me."

"Please explain."

"People want to feel like they know me. I'm their hero, after all. Well, I can't go out and meet everyone, so the best I can do is sell them things with my face and name on them. For instance, my company sells Woodcutter Three-Bean Chili, Woodcutter Toilet Cakes, Woodcutter Beef Jerky, Woodcutter Steel-Belted Radial Tires, Woodcutter Diaper Rash Powder—the list goes on and on. I also operate an amusement park, and of course, the Howard Hatchett Historical Museum located right here in Ferryport Landing. I'm currently seeking investors for my latest venture—a chain of Woodcutter Home-Cooking Restaurants."

"How did you become this hero to millions?" the lawyer asked.

Hatchett glanced at Canis one last time. Sabrina watched his confusion turn to confidence, as if a great weight had been lifted from his shoulders. "Well, it was sort of thrust on me. One day I was out in the forest and I heard a scream. I was just a regular working stiff back then, you know, just like everybody. I never thought of myself as a hero, but there are those who stand by and watch and a rare few who act. So, with nothing more than my wits and my ax, I raced off to help."

"What did you find?" Bluebeard said, sounding inspired.

"I came upon a little house in the woods. Inside, there was this terrible shouting. I peered into the window and saw a monster attacking a child. Well, I suppose a normal person might have just run off, but I'm not normal. I knew people were in trouble. I knew I would fight to the death to save them."

"You say you saw a monster. Do you see that monster in the courtroom today?"

Hatchett looked over at Canis, and for a moment, the man's confidence dissolved. He pointed with a trembling hand at the old man. "It was him."

"Let the record show that Mr. Hatchett is referring to the accused," Bluebeard said, then turned his attention back to Hatchett. "You mean the Wolf. Were you afraid?" Bluebeard continued.

Hatchett shook his head. "When you're a man like me, you go to a place where fear doesn't follow. I look back on it now and I laugh. I should have been afraid."

"Oh, brother," Puck said.

The crowd turned to glare at him.

"Please, could he be any more dramatic?"

Judge Hatter slammed his desk with the sledgehammer, sending a portion of the wood to the floor. "Silence in the courtroom!"

"What happened next?" Bluebeard continued.

"I pounded on the door so hard it fell off its hinges. I'm a strong guy. I work out. I can bench about two-fifty, really. Then I rushed in with my ax raised. The Wolf had finished off the old woman—there was nothing I could do for her, but the little girl was still in danger. Now the monster knew he didn't want to go head to head with me, so in desperation he turned and swallowed the little girl whole."

Mr. Canis shifted uncomfortably.

"Good heavens!" Bluebeard cried. "What did you do?"

"That's a situation where instinct takes over. I swung my ax at the monster's belly. It split from end to end and the child spilled out, perfectly healthy. The assault caused the Wolf to pass out, so I filled his belly full of rocks and sewed it shut with some thread I found in a cabinet. Then I carried the creature on my back to the river and tossed him in. The weight of the rocks caused him to sink to the bottom."

"Yet he lived," Bluebeard said, gesturing at Canis.

"He's a tough customer," Hatchett replied. "But I'm tougher."

"I appreciate your time," Bluebeard replied as he took his seat. "I'm finished with this witness."

Hatchett barely noticed. He continued promoting himself. "I tell the whole story on my Web site, hatchettland.com. It's a great place to buy my various products, including my twelve-inch action figure with kung-fu grip, my Woodcutter All-Protein Organic Cereal Bars, Woodcutter Toilet Paper, Woodcutter Nasal Spray, and the new six-patty Hatchett EZ-Grill. It seals in the juices and drains the fat for perfect burgers every time!"

Robin Hood leaped to his feet. "I have some questions for you!" he shouted as he approached the man.

"Order!" the judge cried, but Robin ignored him.

"You claimed you saw a monster attack the women—can you be sure it was the Wolf?"

"Order!"

"How did you carry his huge body over your shoulder, filled with stones no less, and dump it in the river? How far away was this river? Did anyone see you do this?"

"Order! Order! Order! " the judge shrieked.

"I have the right to question witnesses, your honor!" the lawyer shouted.

"Objection!" Bluebeard cried.

Hatter slammed the heavy sledgehammer down on his desk, which split into two and collapsed. "Now look what you've made me do!"

"This trial is a sham!" Little John shouted, as he leaped to his feet.

"Guards, remove these men from my sight!" the judge demanded. A mob of card soldiers rushed forward and pulled Robin Hood and Little John from the courtroom, but they didn't go peacefully. They fought and shouted that there was no justice in Ferryport Landing.

When they were gone, Judge Hatter got to his feet. "We'll see you all here tomorrow." He left, and the crowd started filing out of the courtroom. Guards dragged Canis out of the courtroom and back to his cell.

Granny rushed everyone outside, where they found Robin Hood and Little John crawling out of the gutter and dusting themselves off. Sabrina expected the men to be furious but they were both laughing.

"It's been a while since we got thrown out of a place, hasn't it, old friend?" Robin said.

Little John laughed. "McSorley threw us out of his pub last week, Robin."

"Oh, yeah, I forgot!" The men roared with laughter.

"You two seem to be in a good mood," Granny said.

"Actually, we're in a rotten mood," Little John replied. "But it's important to laugh from time to time. As for this court case, well, it's a joke. They aren't going to let Canis defend himself."

"Our approach now is to cause as much of a disturbance as possible," Robin Hood said.

"I'd like to help with that," Puck offered.

"You'll get your chance soon enough, Trickster King," Robin said.

"What do you have in mind?" Uncle Jake asked.

"Oh, that would be telling," Robin said. "As for now, I think I'd like to take a visit to Mr. Hatchett's amusement park. I have a feeling that he's not telling the whole story."

"You think he was lying?" Daphne asked.

"That scrawny little man couldn't carry a sack of groceries on his back, let alone the Big Bad Wolf," Little John replied. "If only we could let Canis out, I have a feeling he could get the man to confess a few things he'd rather keep secret."

"We don't need the Wolf for that," Daphne said. "Can we stop at home for a second before we go see Hatchett?"

"Sure, *liebling*," Granny said. "What do you have in mind?"

• • •

Granny and Daphne rushed into the house. Sabrina waited in the car and watched the light flash on in Mirror's room. They must have been picking up something in the Hall of Wonders. When they returned, they explained their plan to the rest of the group.

Puck was ecstatic. "It's been a while since I've had the opportunity to pull a good prank," the boy crowed.

"You filled my pillow with horse manure four days ago," Sabrina reminded him.

"Four days is a long time," he replied.

Robin Hood and Little John pulled up outside the house and honked the horn.

"That's them," Granny said. "Let's go."

Uncle Jake backed the car out of the driveway, made sure the lawyers were right behind him, and then drove the family through the country roads of Ferryport Landing. Granny navigated with the help of a tattered map.

"I didn't know anything about an amusement park dedicated to the Red Riding Hood story," Uncle Jake said.

"Years ago Dr. Doolittle ran a petting zoo on the property, but it went bankrupt when the animals went on strike," Granny said. "Apparently, Hatchett bought up the land. I have to wonder how much money he makes on the place. It's out in the middle of nowhere, and, to be honest, I hadn't heard a word about it until this morning."

"Well, we're about to find out," Uncle Jake said, pointing ahead. "There it is."

The amusement park looked more like a shrine to Hatchett than a place for a family to spend the day. A twenty-five-foot-tall statue of Hatchett himself greeted everyone at the front entrance. To get into the parking lot, the cars had to drive between the statue's legs. Uncle Jake pulled the car through just as it backfired and sent a cloud of black smoke upward, staining the statue's pants. In the parking lot they found a dozen more statues of Hatchett, including one where he stood triumphantly over a cowering wolf.

"This guy sure does love himself," Little John said as he and Robin got out of their car.

"He's the idol of millions, remember?" Sabrina said sarcastically.

"How do we get in?" Puck asked.

Uncle Jake pointed to a path with a sign above it that read THIS WAY TO THE SCENE OF THE CRIME!

The group followed the path until they came to a gate with several turnstile entrances. To the right was a store. A sign above it read THE BIG BAD GIFT SHOP. Sabrina spotted movement through one of the store's windows and led everyone inside. Her entrance triggered a mechanical wolf's howl that came from a dusty speaker mounted above the door. A pimply faced teenager behind the counter put down his handheld video game and approached the group. When he reached them, Sabrina noticed he was wearing a hat with big wolf ears on it.

"Welcome to Hatchettland," he said in a well-rehearsed voice. "Are you here to visit the museum or just stopping by to stock up on all our popular Woodcutter-brand products like our gourmet Woodcutter Wasabi?"

"Actually, we were hoping we could have a word with Mr. Hatchett himself," Granny said.

"He's down at the house," the teenager said.

"The house?" Sabrina asked.

"It's at the end of the path. If you want to see him, you have to buy tickets."

Granny sighed but purchased enough tickets to get everyone into the park. Once past the turnstiles they saw a sign that read

WHERE IT ALL HAPPENED. GRANNY'S HOUSE! They hurried down a dirt path surrounded by forest. As they walked, speakers attached to trees told the story of Little Red Riding Hood and how Hatchett's bravery had saved her life and the lives of countless others. The speakers crackled loudly, giving Sabrina a major headache.

At the end of the path there was a small wooden shack with a brick chimney. It looked rundown and drafty, with broken windows and vines growing up the walls to the roof. At odds with its appearance was the bright, blinking neon sign above its door that read GRANNY'S HOUSE.

"What's this?" Sabrina asked.

Hatchett stepped through the front door. He looked startled to find the group waiting for him, but he quickly composed himself and gestured at the meager building.

"This is the house," Hatchett announced.

"What house?"

"*The* house. This is where it all happened. This is Red Riding Hood's grandmother's house."

"You built a model of it?" Uncle Jake asked.

"No, this is the actual house. I had it disassembled and shipped piece by piece to Ferryport Landing," he said.

"Whatever for?" Granny asked.

"'Cause this is a bona fide, moneymaking tourist attraction.

Do you know how many people know the story of Red Riding Hood? People read about it in every nation of the world and there are a lot of them that would pay a pretty penny to visit the actual place. Want to go inside?"

Sabrina wasn't sure. If the stories were true, then horrible things had happened inside the little shack. It gave her chills just thinking about it, but Hatchett wouldn't take no for an answer. He opened the door and urged everyone to come inside.

The house was one room with a dirt floor. There was a crude table and a chair in the corner and a small bed on the other side of the room. A dressing gown lay on a tattered quilt on the bed. The fireplace was ablaze and a cast-iron pot hung above the flames. Other than the fire, the room was dark, and the firelight created shadows that slithered along the walls. Sabrina was completely unnerved. She imagined she heard distant screams echoing around the room, until she realized the screams were real and coming from a speaker in the corner of the room.

"Every time I come in here, it's like I'm transported to that day," Hatchett said.

"Good to know," Little John said. "'Cause we've got some questions about it."

"I've said all I'm going to say on this matter. If you want to know more, you can read my book. It's called *Facing the Fangs:*

One Man's Journey into the Jaws of Death. It's for sale in the gift shop. It got a starred review from *Publishers Weekly.*"

"Congratulations," Robin Hood said. "But we don't have time to read your book. A man's life is in jeopardy."

"I'm sorry, Mr. Hood." Hatchett said. "I wish I could give you details, but the truth is it was a very long time ago. All that I really remember is that it changed me into the man I am today. When you become a hero, the little things just aren't that important."

"I had a feeling you would say that," Granny said. "Children, would you like to step outside and get some air?"

Sabrina recognized the code the group had worked out beforehand. It was time to get down to business and Puck couldn't have been more excited. He dragged the girls out of the shack and closed the door behind him.

"Oh boy, oh boy, oh boy! This is going to be so much fun!" Puck shouted.

Daphne took a long, thin wand from her purse. It had a shiny silver star at the end. "Don't worry, this won't hurt at all."

"Will it make me strong like the Wolf?"

"Sorry," Daphne said. "Fairy Godmother wands don't work like that. You'll just look like him; you won't have any of his powers."

"Or his twisted desires, so don't try and eat anyone," Sabrina added.

"You're no fun," Puck replied. "If only I could do this without a wand—boy, the trouble I could get into. I can shape shift into a wolf on my own, but old Big and Bad is his own breed; I'd never be able to do it justice. How long will this last?"

"I'm giving you ten minutes," Daphne said. "After that you'll be back to your old self, so don't goof off. We need to get him talking and fast."

"Lay it on me, sister," Puck said.

Daphne flicked the wand and smacked Puck on the head. The boy winced. "I thought you said this wouldn't hurt!" But before he could complain any further, a change came over him. Hair sprouted from every pore. Fangs grew in his mouth. Talons popped out of his fingers and toes. He grew several feet and put on hundreds of pounds of muscle. Seconds later, his transformation was complete. He looked exactly like the Big Bad Wolf.

"Did it work?" Puck asked as he peered down at himself.

"You look just like him," Sabrina said with a shudder. She was still handcuffed to Puck, and his new shape made her recoil in fear. She had to take several deep breaths to calm down.

"All right, let's go introduce you to Hatchett," Daphne said as she put away the wand.

Puck nodded. "Wait, let me roar. He'll lose his mind if I roar." Puck let out a long, goofy howl that sounded nothing like a wolf.

"You might want to skip the howl," Sabrina said.

"Everyone's a critic," Puck complained.

The children entered the little house. Instantly, Hatchett fell to the floor, scampered into a corner, and screamed like a baby.

"Remember me?" Puck growled, pushing Hatchett down with his paws.

"How did you get out of jail?" Granny cried, though her acting left a lot to be desired.

"No jail can hold me. I'm the Big Bad Wolf. The only person meaner than me is Puck, the Trickster King," Puck said. "That kid is mean. But I'm running a close second."

Sabrina kicked him in the leg. "Cool it, fairy boy."

"What do you want from me?" Hatchett cried.

"Oh, I don't know, a leg bone would be nice," Puck said, attempting his goofy roar again.

"Tobias!" Hatchett said. "Get ahold of yourself. Fight the monster, Tobias. It's me, Howard!"

"Who's Tobias?" Little John asked.

"You're Tobias, Tobias Clay," Hatchett jabbered to the Wolf. "You're a woodcutter. You hired me to be your apprentice. You're a good man. Please don't eat me!"

Puck looked to the family and even in his Wolf form he looked confused. Sabrina knew how he felt.

"Maybe if you tell us the truth the Wolf will have some mercy," Uncle Jake stammered, obviously trying to sustain the illusion.

"The truth! Yes, I'll tell the truth. Tobias and I were working in the forest collecting wood for the local mill. I had only been working for him for a few weeks, but I was already surpassing his skill." Puck growled.

"OK! You were about to fire me. I was goofing off, taking breaks, and making you do all the work. You had given me one last chance, but I didn't care," Hatchett said. "I hated cutting down trees.

"We were working in one of the darker parts of the forest when we heard a scream. You wanted to go check it out but I told you to forget about it. The woods were dangerous. It could have been anything—bandits, witches, goblins. I told you we would be fools to investigate, but you wouldn't listen. So we tramped through the forest until we came upon the house. There was a horrible storm directly above it. I was sure the house was going to blow away."

"So what did you do?" Daphne said. "And don't lie. Our friend hasn't had his lunch yet, you know."

Hatchett squealed and trembled, but he continued. "Tobias dragged me to the hut and we looked inside. There was the old woman, and one look at her was all I needed to know she was a witch."

"A witch?" Robin cried.

"That can't be!" Granny shouted.

"It's true! She was shouting and screaming and blowing into this little flute. Every time she did a wind broke out in the room, blowing everything this way and that. It was almost like she was standing in the middle of a tornado, but she was untouched. In fact, there was only one other thing in the room that wasn't in danger—a rabid wolf inside a steel cage.

"The wolf was snarling and howling. You could tell it was sick because it was foaming at the mouth. You saw a lot of these animals out in the forest back then. I'd learned to steer clear of them. Rabies causes a madness to come over them, and if they bite you it can infect you as well."

"What was she doing to the wolf?" Robin asked.

"It's still hard to describe, but she was kind of splitting the animal into two pieces," Hatchett explained.

"Gross!" Daphne exclaimed.

"Not physically!" Hatchett said. "The wind seemed to be pulling the madness out of the animal . . . like she was taking the bad stuff out of it. She pulled the wolf's dark self out of it and it was now its own animal. It was made out of shadows and viciousness. The old woman trapped it in a clay jar and put a stopper on it. Then the wind faded as if it had never been there. Once it was gone, the wolf in the cage was as tame as a golden retriever."

"Get to the point!" Puck growled, bearing his wolf fangs. "We don't care about some regular wolf. When did I show up?"

"Let him finish, Puck . . . I mean, Wolf," Uncle Jake said.

"Back then magic was something people feared, so I begged Tobias to leave. We were getting set to go and get some help when the little girl arrived."

"Red Riding Hood?" Robin asked.

Hatchett nodded. "She came skipping up to the house and knocked on the door. The witch told her to come inside and she did. They hugged and I realized the witch was the child's grandmother. A moment later, the old woman was helping the child into one of the empty cages and turning her wind machine on. That's when Tobias decided to act. He was really brave. He didn't give it a second thought. He just stormed into the house and attacked the witch. I'd never seen anything like it. They fought like animals until Tobias knocked that clay jar out of the witch's hand. It shattered on the ground and then—well, you wanted to know when the Big Bad Wolf showed up? That's when it happened."

"I'm confused, Howard," Granny said. "That's when what happened?"

"The madness that was inside the wolf wrapped itself around Tobias. It seemed to seep into his pores and a moment later my boss was gone and the Big Bad Wolf was born."

"Red's grandmother created the Big Bad Wolf?" Daphne asked.

Hatchett nodded. "The witch's spell transformed him into the monster. After that, Tobias didn't exist anymore, it was only the Wolf. He was like that for a long time, until fifteen years ago, when I heard he had regained control."

Sabrina reached into her pocket and felt the energy of the kazoo. She realized the tiny object had big secrets, more than she had originally suspected.

"Then what happened to the grandmother?" Puck asked.

"She fought him as hard as she could. There were so many spells coming out of her, but none seemed to hurt the Wolf. He just kept coming and she was no match for him," Hatchett said, then looked into Puck's face. "I mean, she was no match for you. What else can I tell you?"

"Did you even fight the Wolf?" Daphne asked.

"No, I hid," Hatchett whimpered. "After a little while when I was sure the Wolf was gone, I stumbled upon the child. I took her back to her village, but her family was gone. They had deserted her, so I took her to the local sheriff."

"And that's when you made up the story of how you had saved her," Sabrina said, disgusted.

"I figured what could it hurt? The child was out of her mind anyway. She would repeat whatever I told her."

"You took advantage of a little girl who had just witnessed her grandmother's murder," Little John bellowed. "What she saw drove her insane!"

The thought of having to deal with the huge lawyer, as well as the Wolf, was obviously too much for Hatchett and he broke down into tears.

"That's not my fault. She was crazy when she showed up at the house! You could see it in her face. Even the witch was afraid of her. "

Robin tapped Puck on his huge shoulders. "Let him up."

"Aw, c'mon," Puck said. "I don't think he even wet his pants."

As Hatchett climbed to his feet, Puck's disguise began to fade. The would-be hero watched with alarm. "What is this?"

"Sorry, but the hands of justice are unfair in this town," said Robin. "We've had to learn to play dirty, too. What you've told us is going to be a great help to our case."

Hatchett turned red with anger. "No one will believe you! I'll lie. I'll tell them you're making it up. I'm a hero. They'll believe me."

"I'm sure you're right," Robin said as he reached into his jacket pocket. When he removed his hand, he was holding a small tape recorder. "That's why I brought this." He pressed the stop button and then rewound it, playing back Hatchett's confession.

"I'll look like a fool! I'll be ruined!"

"Mr. Hatchett, you do quite a good job of that all on your own," Granny said. "You are a charlatan who has lied his way into fame and fortune. If I were you, I'd change my ways, because I know the real Big Bad Wolf, and he's not as nice as Puck."

Hatchett rushed out of the shack.

"Do you realize what we have here?" Robin said, waving his tape recorder in the air. "We now have proof that Canis didn't mean to kill the old woman. In fact, we might even be able to argue that the old woman is responsible for all the mayhem the Wolf has created. She literally unleashed the Wolf on the world."

"But will it matter?" Sabrina asked.

§

At the end of another long day, after Uncle Jake dashed off for a late dinner with Briar Rose, Granny suggested everyone else get some sleep. She was sure tomorrow would be a big day in Mr. Canis's trial, perhaps even the day their old friend would be freed. The girls and Puck said goodnight to Granny and Elvis and climbed the steps to their bedrooms. The girls said goodnight to Puck at their door. He grunted and kept walking down the hall. Unfortunately, Sabrina was dragged along with him.

"Oh, I forgot about you," Puck said, eyeing the handcuffs.

"What are we supposed to do, fairy boy?" Sabrina cried. "We're not sleeping in the same bed."

"Who cares about that? I'm going to have to go to the bathroom eventually," Puck mumbled.

"He could sleep on the floor in our room," Daphne said.

"I'm not sleeping on the floor. I'm royalty," Puck declared as he puffed up his chest. "Sabrina can sleep there."

"That's not going to happen," Sabrina said.

Puck huffed and frowned. "Fine, come with me."

He led the girls down the hallway to his bedroom. The door was covered in signs: DEATH AWAITS ALL WHO ENTER HERE! and WARNING! FALLING ROCKS! There was also a picture of a kitten, with the words CUTENESS WILL NOT BE SPARED! Puck pushed open the door and impatiently ushered them inside.

Sabrina had been in Puck's room before, but it never ceased to amaze her. It wasn't like any bedroom she had ever seen. The night sky was the roof, the forest ground the floor, and a trickling brook led to a lagoon in the distance. The chirping of crickets and the rustle of woodland animals drifted across the air like a lullaby. The room was magical, and from what Sabrina could tell, endless. Who knew how far the water rolled downstream? If you followed it, would you find an ocean at its end? Sabrina didn't know, though she wondered about it from time to time.

Puck dragged the girls down to where the room's serene beauty came to a dismaying end. There they found a path littered with broken army men and parts from old skateboards and microwaves. Sabrina nearly stepped into dozens of half-eaten birthday cakes.

They climbed up an embankment, where they found a trampoline. A panda bear was sound asleep on its surface. Puck shooed it away. It staggered off, looking for somewhere else to sleep, barking and growling grumpily with each step.

Puck helped Daphne onto the trampoline, then Sabrina, and together the girls pulled him up behind them.

"I love it," Daphne said, jumping up and down and bouncing like a ball.

"Good to know," Puck grumbled. "My only concern is making sure the two of you are comfortable. Now, go to sleep and leave me alone."

Puck lay down, forcing Sabrina to do the same. She nudged as far away from him as possible, feeling entirely uncomfortable. Daphne nestled between them, her head at the tips of their fingers. The handcuffs forced them to sleep on their backs. It was hard to get comfortable, and each time Sabrina drifted to sleep she felt Puck's hand drag her hand this way and that. Eventually she decided that despite her best efforts, sleeping was out of the question. Instead, she settled on resting. She closed her eyes and lay still, listening to the bubbling water in the distance.

"You awake?" Puck asked.

"Yes," Sabrina said. Their voices seemed loud in the open air.

"When are you going to tell her what you did?"

Sabrina bristled. "Maybe you should mind your own business."

Puck laughed. "As if I could around this place. Every time I turn around the two of you are facing down death—monsters, robots, dragons. Saving your butts is a full-time job."

His tone made her angrier. "Then why don't you go back to being a villain? I liked you a lot better when you weren't trying to save us."

"I'll go back to being a villain if you go back to the way you were," Puck said.

"And how was I, Mr. Smarty Pants?"

"For one, you were honest," Puck said.

The words were like a smack in the face and her cheeks grew hot. Who was he to tell her how to be a good person? Wasn't his name the Trickster King? He'd been treating people like chumps for four thousand years. "You're one to talk."

Puck chuckled. "I am a lot of things, Sabrina—mischievous, mean-spirited, gassy—but they don't make me a bad person. They make me immature. You, however, are skating very close to the line. You stole from someone who trusted you and then you lied about it."

Sabrina wanted to get up and storm away, but she knew the handcuffs wouldn't let her. She was forced to hear his sermon about good and bad, no matter how ridiculous it sounded.

"I did what I had to do. Daphne would never have gone to

get the weapon. Mr. Canis could eat Granny, Elvis, and half of Ferryport Landing and she would still totally trust him. I'm the only one that sees what he's becoming."

"Who's arguing with you about that? It's obvious to most of us that furface is in trouble. I won't even say you're wrong about wanting to do something about it."

"Then what's the lecture for?"

"The lecture's beause the way you are going about these things kinda stinks. It's all nice and noble of you to want to do the right thing, even if I do think it's stupid. But if the only way to make something good happen is to do something bad, then maybe it's not worth it."

Sabrina looked off into the dark forest, not wanting to see Puck's face.

"But what do I know? I'm not supposed to be a good person. But you are. You're Sabrina Grimm and your sister worships you. You're supposed to be a good role model to her. Don't you think it's kind of odd that the Prince of Juvenile Delinquents is teaching you right from wrong?"

Sabrina mulled over Puck's words as she lay in the dark. She wondered if he might not be right. She knew she had betrayed her sister, but at the same time she realized that she didn't really care about Daphne's opinion. She had been in charge of the two of them ever since their parents disappeared and things had worked out just fine. If she had let Daphne vote on their futures, the two of them would be in a heap of trouble.

"By the way," Puck said softly. It had been an hour since he had last spoken and she was startled to hear him still awake. "You don't need the makeup."

Sabrina felt like her face was on fire. He knew about her late-night beauty sessions. And, if she had heard him correctly, he was also admitting that he thought she was pretty. She looked over at him and found he was looking at her.

"I kinda wish I hadn't said that," he said.

"Me, too," she replied.

"Would it help if I said you were a stinky, muck-covered toad-face?"

Sabrina nodded and edged as far away as she could on the trampoline. Puck did the same.

• • •

"Hello!" Uncle Jake's voice echoed from near the lagoon.

"We're here!" Sabrina shouted as she sat up, taking Puck with her. Together they shook Daphne awake.

"Come on! I found our mysterious Goldilocks again. She's in Paris."

When the children followed their uncle into Mirror's room,

they found Briar Rose sitting on the bed next to their sleeping parents. She barely had time to say hello before an excited Jake flew into an explanation of why he had woken them.

"As you know, Goldilocks hopped on a flight out of Venice as quickly as possible," Uncle Jake said as he stood before the mirror. Behind him, the children could see images of Paris. Sabrina marveled at its majestic architecture. The city seemed to be a combination of timeless beauty and modern design. "Whoever that man on the motorcycle was, she's obviously frightened of him. Luckily, we don't have to go to all the trouble of tracking her down again. Mirror showed me an exact address. She's checked into a place called the Hotel Thérèse."

"Then we don't have to go back to the library with that book-tossing idiot?" Puck said, as he began to scratch himself at the memory.

"Not at all. We can go straight to her," Uncle Jake said.

"Well, what are we waiting for?" Sabrina asked as she stepped toward the traveler's chest.

"Uh, when I said we, I didn't mean you," Uncle Jake said.

"What? Why?" Sabrina asked.

"You happen to be handcuffed to an Everafter, and as we know, Everafters can't leave the town. You're going to have to stay here with Puck and Briar," Uncle Jake explained.

Sabrina could have strangled the fairy boy. Especially when he smirked at her. "But I can go?" Daphne asked.

Uncle Jake nodded. "Yes, but you'll have to stay close to me. It could be dangerous." He reached into his pocket and handed the little girl a key. "You want to give it a whirl this time?"

Daphne looked at it like it was a precious jewel. She repeated the address Uncle Jake told her, then inserted the key. When she turned it, the lid opened, revealing a spiral staircase.

"I'm so jealous!" Briar said. "I haven't been to Paris in hundreds of years."

"We'll bring you back a souvenir," Daphne said.

Uncle Jake took his girlfriend by the hand. "If I could take you with me—"

Briar kissed him on the cheek. "Don't talk to any French girls."

Uncle Jake winked at Briar, then turned to Daphne. "Let's scoot!"

Sabrina was livid but forced a smile to her face. "Be careful," she told her sister.

"I'll be fine," the little girl said impatiently, and rolled her eyes.

A moment later, she and Uncle Jake were gone.

"He said we could watch them from the magic mirror," Briar said.

Mirror's face appeared in the reflection. "Hello, ladies and gentlemen. What can I show you this evening?"

"We want to watch Uncle Jake and Daphne in Paris," Sabrina said.

"Coming right up," Mirror replied. "Just say the magic words."

"Mirror, Mirror for goodness sake, let me watch Daphne and Uncle Jake."

Mirror smiled. "That's more like it." His face dissolved and the mirror's surface revealed a narrow avenue lined with elegant apartment buildings. Each building had a smoky bar, or a cozy restaurant, or a little boutique on its ground level. People were spilling out of all of them, drinking wine and gazing to the heavens. High above, fireworks filled the sky. Streams of blues, greens, reds, and whites shot across the horizon, then fizzled before the next round. In the distance, an enormous steel tower hovered above it all. It was illuminated by thousands of little lights, and at its top a beacon flashed a brilliant spotlight three hundred and sixty degrees.

Sabrina turned to Briar to gauge her reaction. The woman was awestruck. "That's the Eiffel Tower," she said. "It's amazing."

Sabrina suddenly realized what Briar must feel. She had been trapped for more than two hundred years in a little town. Now, all at once, she could see the outside world so vividly it seemed real. Paris was a place, Sabrina suspected, Briar never expected to see again.

Uncle Jake and Daphne stepped out of a doorway and gaped at their surroundings. They stood still for a moment in awe of the city.

"There she is!" Briar said, pointing at a woman walking down the street. Sabrina searched the crowd. It was indeed Goldilocks, their elusive savior. She was grinning from ear to ear, obviously enjoying the sights and sounds of the city of lights.

"She's there, Jake!" Briar cried.

"Sorry, he can't hear you," Sabrina said. "It doesn't work like that."

"How frustrating," Briar complained.

Luckily, Uncle Jake seemed to spot Goldilocks as well, and they watched him and Daphne follow the woman down the street.

"I'm not sure how she's going to react," Puck said. "If they asked me to come back here I don't think I would. They'd have to stuff me in a sack and drag me back against my will."

Sabrina was unnerved by Puck's words. She had never once thought that Goldilocks might not want to come back to Ferryport Landing, but the more it spun around in her head, the more troubling the idea became. Why would she want to come back? The town was controlled by the Scarlet Hand. She

would be trapped inside the barrier again. Her true love was married with children, and from a letter of Goldilocks's that Sabrina had read, the woman seemed to believe she was responsible for the death of their grandfather, Basil Grimm. If the roles were switched, would Sabrina return? She realized the answer was no. An army couldn't drag her back to this horrible little place. What would they do if Goldilocks refused?

Just then, a black motorcycle tore down the street. The hair on the back of Sabrina's neck stood on end. The driver was the same man they had seen in Venice—the same man who was terrorizing Goldilocks.

"What's going on? Who's that?" Briar asked.

"That dude in black is following her everywhere," Sabrina explained. "He's one of the Scarlet Hand."

Sabrina watched her sister and uncle bolt down the street, weaving in and out of pedestrians and knocking a waiter carrying coffee cups to the ground. Sabrina shouted for them to be careful, knowing full well they couldn't hear her. Still, it made her feel better to try.

Goldilocks spun around in the street. She must have spotted the motorcyclist, because she quickly hailed a taxicab and got inside—moments later she and the cab were roaring away.

"If we were there we could track her by air," Puck said.

Sabrina nodded. She should be there, helping her sister, making sure she was safe. She felt an incredible anxiety rip through her. She realized that this was the first time she and Daphne had been separated in a very long time. Daphne could be injured. This lunatic on the motorcycle might hurt her. Anything could happen.

Briar seemed to sense her fear. She reached out and squeezed Sabrina's hand. "They'll be fine, Sabrina."

Sabrina nodded and watched Daphne and Uncle Jake jump into their own taxi in hot pursuit. With the image focused on her family, Sabrina couldn't see Goldilocks, but she saw the motorcycle race past their cab. She watched Daphne roll down the window and crane her neck out to see where he was headed. When the cab made a sudden turn, she nearly fell out and Sabrina screamed.

"That was a close one," Puck laughed but stopped when both Sabrina and Briar flashed him an angry look. "What? It was funny."

Suddenly, like water flowing from a broken dam, a herd of stray dogs poured out of every alley and doorway. There were rottweilers, German shepherds, Doberman pinschers, pit bulls, wolfhounds, beagles, poodles, golden retrievers, Shih Tzus, West Highland white terriers, and dozens more in hot pursuit. They barked and snapped at the black-clad rider's feet, causing him to swerve all over the road.

"She's called some friends," Sabrina said.

"She can talk to animals?" Puck said. "That rules."

The dogs gave the rider as much trouble as they could, but his bike was faster than all of them. Soon, they were left behind, causing traffic to back up all over Paris. Luckily, Uncle Jake and Daphne's cab was undeterred and their driver raced on, steering the car into a circular street called Place Charles de Gaulle. At its center was an elegant arch decorated with statues and finely carved reliefs. Cars whipped around the circle from all directions. Without any traffic lights or signs, the circle was pure chaos, and there were several times Sabrina was sure her family would die in a head-on collision. But the driver was quick, and he steered the car out of traffic at the last possible second and darted down a tree-lined road bordering a park.

"Where do you think she's going?" Sabrina wondered aloud.

"Exactly where I'd go," Briar said, pointing at the approaching metal tower rising like a giant on the Parisian horizon—the Eiffel Tower. The tower was an incredible work of engineering made from huge steel girders and stood more than a thousand feet tall. It was quite a bit bigger than Sabrina had imagined, and she suddenly felt envious of her sister for seeing it in person without her.

Sabrina watched Uncle Jake and Daphne's cab come to a stop.

They paid the driver and leaped out just in time to watch Goldilocks dashing toward the entrance to the tower.

"Why would she go up there?" Briar said. "There's no way off that thing once she gets to the top."

"She's probably going to pull the talking animal stunt again. When we tracked her down in Venice, she had a bunch of pigeons fly her to safety. I bet she wants motorcycle boy to follow her up there so she can do the same thing. It would be a great way to lose him."

"Except I doubt it will work. The wind has to be crazy powerful up there," Puck said. "I don't think my wings could take it. I doubt a bird could do it, either."

Sabrina gasped. "So there's no way off that thing if he catches her?"

Puck shook his head. "Not unless your uncle and sister can rescue her from that lunatic."

"Speak of the devil," Briar said as they watched the deadly motorcyclist skid to a stop nearby. He leaped off his bike and pulled a silver dagger from his boot; then he raced through the entrance to the tower. Sabrina saw Daphne pointing at the motorcycle. Without a word, she dashed through the entrance to the tower. Uncle Jake tossed the entrance fee to a clerk, and he and Daphne hurried into an elevator, just as it was about to shut. Sabrina scanned the tightly packed crowd around them. The man in black wasn't there, but neither was Goldilocks. She imagined the poor woman, standing at the top, backing away from the dark rider with his deadly blade. She tried to force the vision out of her head. They would get there in time. They had to.

They reached the first of the tower's three platforms and tumbled out of the elevator. Daphne pointed at a sign leading to the elevator that would take them to the next level. She and Uncle Jake pushed through the crowd and made their way onto the next elevator. Soon, they were rising even higher above the Paris skyline.

The second level was much higher, and a few people lost their hats in the strong wind. Puck had been right. Nature's forces were brutal at that height, and it wasn't even the top of the tower.

"Look!" Puck cried as the mirror's reflection showed the murderous motorcyclist entering the final elevator. Sabrina could almost hear the chaos when he pulled out his dagger and demanded that everyone get off. People nearly trampled one another to get away from the mad man. She watched him push a button and the doors closed, just as her sister and uncle approached. The two Grimms could only stare as the elevator rose to the top of the tower where Goldilocks had fled.

Sabrina watched the rising elevator. It disappeared from view for several moments. The ascent to the top would take a long time. By the time it came back down, who knew what the villain might have accomplished. It wasn't fair! Somebody had to stop him.

"There will be another one," Briar said to Sabrina. "Don't worry."

But she was wrong. Suddenly, the elevator came crashing down from above. People were screaming and smoke filled the air.

"Daphne! Uncle Jake!" Sabrina cried frantically, but quickly spotted them. Daphne had fallen, but Uncle Jake helped her up. Together they studied the wreckage. The man in black had somehow cut the cables.

"He's diabolical," Briar said.

"And not in the good way," Puck replied.

"There's no way up to the top," Sabrina said. "They'll never get to her in time. Goldilocks is up there, alone. He's going to kill her!"

"If only I could go," Briar said, reaching into her pocket and removing a small seed. "With one of these I could get Jacob to the top in a flash."

"Uh, I'm glad you are so excited about gardening, Briar, but we've got an emergency on our hands," Sabrina said.

"No, let me explain. When I was a kid, a witch put a spell on me that said if I ever pricked my finger on a spinning wheel I would die. Well, luckily I had a couple of fairy godmothers and they fixed the spell so I would fall asleep. To keep me safe from wild animals and nutcases, they also created a magical rosebush that covered the castle so no one could get at me. When William Charming managed to cut his way through and woke me up, the first thing I did was cultivate some of the rosebush's seeds. The seeds grow like crazy, and they seem to understand how I want them to grow, too. They come in handy from time to time. All you need is a handful of dirt."

"I have a handful of dirt," Puck said, reaching into his filthy pants pocket. When he pulled out his fist, he had a handful of crumbly soil. A fat earthworm was squiggling in the dirt.

"You carry dirt with you?" Sabrina asked.

"Sure, doesn't everyone?" Puck replied.

"What good is this going to do? We're in Ferryport Landing. The trouble is half a world away! Unless I can get out of these handcuffs, Goldilocks is going to die."

Briar and Sabrina turned their gaze to Puck.

"Listen, I swallowed the key," he stammered. "We have to let nature take its course."

Disgusted, Sabrina turned to the mirror. "Mirror, do we have any lock-picking stuff in the Hall of Wonders?"

Mirror's face appeared. "Starfish, I'm increasingly concerned about your life of crime."

"Mirror! It's an emergency!"

Sabrina handed him her set of keys and moments later he returned with a small leather case. Inside were the kind of tools Sabrina had only dreamed about when she and her sister were wards of the state. There were picks of all shapes and sizes, and she tried each one until the handcuff snapped open. Free, she rubbed her sore wrist, and turned to Briar.

"Maybe we should wake your grandmother?" Briar said as she hesitantly handed over her magic seed.

"No time," Sabrina said, and turned to Puck. "Hand over the dirt."

Puck did as he was told and Sabrina approached the traveler's chest.

She knew if she walked down the steps now, she'd wind up outside of the Hotel Thérèse, far from where she needed to be, so she closed the lid and removed the key. "I want to go to the second-floor observation deck of the Eiffel Tower in Paris, France," she said aloud. Then she inserted the key and opened the lid. Inside she found a completely different set of stairs.

"Be careful," Briar said. "And tell your uncle to do the same."

"I will," Sabrina said as she descended. She hurried down the stairs and into the dark until she found the door, but this one did not have a doorknob. Instead, she found a button. She pushed it and it lit up, but nothing happened. She was considering turning back when the door slid open. She immediately saw her sister and uncle.

Sabrina stepped out, realizing she had just gotten out of the elevators on the second level.

"What are you doing here?" Uncle Jake asked.

"Your girlfriend sent me with some help," Sabrina said as she hurried her family to the broken elevator shaft. There she took Puck's dirt and placed it in a heap on the floor. She then took Briar's crusty brown seed and buried it in the small pile of earth. Then she stood up and dusted herself off.

Before she was finished, a tiny green sprout appeared in the dirt. It grew and grew, becoming plump and fat until it was as thick as a tree trunk and covered in roses. In no time it was as tall as Uncle Jake and had pointy thorns sprouting out of its sides.

"My girlfriend is full of secrets," Uncle Jake said as the bush rocketed into the air. He grabbed Daphne in his arms and reached out for a branch. "See you at the top, 'Brina."

A moment later, he was yanked off the ground and sailing skyward as the rosebush grew at an impossible rate. Sabrina grabbed a vine. The strength of the growing bush was incredible. She wondered if her arm might be yanked from the socket, but she held on with all her strength. Sabrina sailed higher and higher and faster and faster until she reached the top of the Eiffel Tower, where the rosebush stopped and the branch eased her gently to the platform.

Sabrina stood for a moment, trying to regain her bearings and feeling the building sway in the powerful wind. She didn't like heights, especially heights moving under her feet.

"She's here!" Daphne cried as she raced across the platform. Goldilocks lay on her back, motionless. Sabrina dashed to her side, with Uncle Jake in tow.

"Is she—?"

"She's alive," Uncle Jake said as he knelt to find a pulse. "It looks like she's unconscious."

"But how?" Sabrina asked.

Her answer came in the sound of running feet. Before anyone could react, the menacing motorcyclist had charged across the platform and tackled Uncle Jake. Caught off guard, Jake was helpless and took several brutal punches to the face and stomach. Sabrina watched him try to defend himself, but the dark rider was fast and fierce.

Sabrina and Daphne rushed to help him, but they were nothing more than mosquitoes to the mysterious villain. He slapped Sabrina with a vicious backhand that sent her tumbling to the floor. When Sabrina righted herself, she realized Daphne was injured as well.

"Uncle Jake!" Sabrina shouted as she watched the two men circle one another. Jake assured her that everything would be fine, but he never took his eyes off the mysterious man.

"You must think you're pretty tough, hitting women and children," Uncle Jake said to the man. He replied by lunging with his knife, slashing and striking out, but Sabrina's uncle was fast and leaped away from every deadly attack.

"And the outfit, hiding your face. Then again, if I were slapping people around who couldn't fight back, I'd want to hide my identity, too."

"You dare question my honor?" a muffled voice said from behind the helmet. "I'm the Black Knight, you fool."

"I thought knights rode horses," Uncle Jake said.

"I upgraded," the Black Knight said.

"Who knighted you?" Uncle Jake said as he continued to dig into his pockets. "That king must have been pretty hard up for heroes."

"I serve no king," the knight growled. "Only the Master and his glorious vision of the future. When Everafters take their place as rulers of the world, your kind will be in cages, serving us."

"Blah, blah, blah," Uncle Jake mocked. "You Scarlet Hand losers sure do love the whole 'we're going to rule the world' bit. It seems to me the only thing you've got power over is my boredom."

"Hold your tongue, fool, or I will cut it from your mouth."

At that moment, Sabrina's uncle took a small ring from his pocket and slipped it on. "Well, pal, if you're feeling froggy, take a leap."

The Black Knight dove for Uncle Jake and the two men toppled over one another. Sabrina watched Jake lock his hand around the knight's wrist, limiting his ability to use his deadly blade. But the knight's other hand was free, and he punched her uncle several times in the jaw. They rolled over each other, kicking and punching along the way. Every time the knight seemed to get the upper hand, Uncle Jake managed to pummel him and gain control, but it never lasted long. The Black Knight was obviously stronger than Uncle Jake and a much better fighter. Sabrina could only watch in horror when the dark villain clenched his free hand around Jake's throat to choke him. Daphne scrambled over once again to lend a hand but was tossed aside. She fell hard on the floor, but her eyes were still open.

"Leave him alone!" Sabrina begged, but the knight ignored her. He continued to squeeze, and Jake's face turned blue. In desperation, he raised his hand to the knight's face, and a blast of red-hot energy exploded out of the tiny ring on his pinky finger. It temporarily blinded Sabrina, but when her eyes adjusted she saw the Black Knight was unfazed.

"My Master has given me a special gift, fool," he said. "Your silly magic won't work on me. Sadly, he won't see your death himself. He so wanted to witness it."

Spittle came out of Uncle Jake's mouth and his eyes started to bulge. The knight was killing him, and there was no one to stop him. No one except for Sabrina. She reached into her pocket, found the kazoo, and aimed it right at the killer. She hoped she could direct its power away from her uncle. Then she blew into it. The wind it produced swirled around the knight like it was a living creature, a bird made of nothingness, circling and howling. It lifted the Black Knight off the floor and in his effort to stay down he released Uncle Jake. The wind carried the knight over the edge of the tower, and he sank out of sight. Sabrina heard his fading screams and rushed to the side of the tower. There, trapped in the vines of the magical rosebush, was the knight. It had saved his life, but it wrapped around his arms and legs to prevent him from escaping.

Sabrina rushed to Uncle Jake's side and helped him sit up. The man's face was raw and red and he coughed violently, but when he got to his feet, Sabrina was sure he would be OK. Daphne raced to the fallen Goldilocks and shouted her name until she woke.

"What happened?" the woman asked.

"Don't worry," Sabrina said, hurrying over. "You're safe. The Black Knight is gone."

"It's you!" she said, her voice higher and more feminine than Sabrina had imagined. She turned to stare at the others until her eyes focused on Jake. She looked startled at first, but then smiled.

"You've come to take me back?" she said, as if in surrender.

Uncle Jake tried to talk but couldn't. All he could do was shake his head.

"We're not here to force you back to Ferryport Landing. We're here to ask you to come back on your own," Sabrina said.

"Who are you?" Goldilocks asked.

"My name is Sabrina Grimm and this is my sister, Daphne," Sabrina said, motioning to the little girl.

"We're Henry Grimm's daughters," Daphne added.

Goldilocks studied their faces. "I see a lot of him in you," she told Daphne, then looked at Sabrina. "So he married that girl, huh? You look just like her."

Sabrina nodded. "Her name is Veronica."

"I know," Goldilocks said as she got to her feet. She turned to Uncle Jake and gave him a hug. "It's good to see you, Jakey."

Uncle Jake nodded and smiled, then pointed at his throat.

"The knight tried to choke him to death," Daphne explained.

"Goldie, you have to come back," Sabrina said. "The town is a disaster and my dad—"

"Tell me he's safe," Goldilocks pleaded. Sabrina could see the woman still felt strongly for her father. She wasn't sure how to react.

"He's fine, but he needs you," Daphne said. "He's under a sleeping spell. We need someone to kiss him. We were told you were the only one who could do that."

Goldilocks blushed. "A kiss from someone who truly loves him is all he needs. Can't you get your mother to do this?"

Sabrina shook her head. "No, she's asleep, too."

"Never a dull moment in Ferryport Landing," the blond beauty said. "How did this happen?"

"The Scarlet Hand did it," Uncle Jake croaked.

"The Scarlet Who?" the blonde asked.

"They're the bad guys," Daphne said. "They kidnapped my parents almost two years ago. Now they are running the town. That creepy guy, the Black Knight, he was one of them."

"He's been chasing me for a month," Goldilocks said. "If he is part of the group that kidnapped your parents, they probably don't want anyone to wake them up. Whoever sent him will send others."

"Come back and we'll protect you," Sabrina said.

Goldilocks looked into Sabrina's face. "Come back to Ferryport Landing?"

Sabrina nodded hopefully.

Goldilocks shook her head. "I can't do that. Terrible things occurred just to set me free. Your grandfather died because of it. Your grandmother doesn't want to see me, and I'm sure Henry wouldn't want to see me, either. He told me to leave him alone."

"But we can't wake him up without you," Daphne begged. "Without you it's impossible."

Goldilocks turned to Uncle Jake. "If I went back, could you set me free again?"

Uncle Jake shook his head. Sabrina wasn't surprised. After what had happened the first time he shut down the barrier, she doubted that her uncle would ever attempt it again. She wondered if he would even do it for Briar.

"Then no," Goldilocks said. "I won't go back. I'm sorry. I wish I could help. Don't give up hope. You live in Ferryport Landing. Anything is possible there." She turned and a moment later she was walking down the steps that led to the second level. Sabrina started to chase after her, but Uncle Jake snatched her arm and pulled her back. He shook his head. "Let her go," he whispered painfully.

"We have to stop her. We can force her to go back with us," Sabrina said.

"That's not what we do," Daphne said, softly. Sabrina noticed Daphne hadn't looked at her since the Black Knight had been thrown from the building.

"But—"

Again, Uncle Jake shook his head. "We'll find another way. It's time to go home."

9

abrina watched her uncle pack up the traveler's chest. An hour later, the same rabbit and tortoise that delivered it came and picked it up. The rabbit hoisted it onto his partner's shell and walked it over to the little truck. Moments later they were gone, along with the only hope the family had of ever seeing Goldilocks again.

"We could go back and change her mind," Sabrina pleaded as the family watched the truck disappear down the road.

"She said no, Sabrina," Jake exclaimed, though speaking still hurt his voice.

"None of you care!" Sabrina raged at her family. "None of you care whether Mom and Dad ever wake up!" She raced upstairs to the room where her parents slept, nestled herself between their bodies, and cried into her hands. Her old thoughts of anger toward Everafters surfaced. Most were betrayers, others couldn't be counted on. She wept openly, not caring if Mirror or anyone else for that matter heard her railing at the world around her. Mirror's face appeared briefly in the reflection but then faded away. She silently thanked him for letting her be alone. She lay there for hours, her face and neck drenched in tears, until eventually she was too exhausted to continue.

After a long while she got to her feet and went out into the hallway. There she found Granny, Uncle Jake, Briar, and Elvis sitting on the hardwood floor, obviously waiting for her. They all had expressions of concern mixed with forced smiles.

Granny took Sabrina by the hand, "Sabrina—"

Sabrina pulled away. "I can't take a lecture right now."

"I was going to say I was sorry. I know how heartbroken you feel. We feel it as well, dear. We had the same hopes that you did."

Sabrina nodded, sadly. "Where's Daphne?"

"She's in your room," the old woman said.

"You might want to leave her alone," Uncle Jake said.

"Why?"

"She's a little angry right now," he replied.

"I know how she feels," Sabrina said, ignoring the warning. She turned and walked down the hall and entered her bedroom. There, she found Daphne sitting at Henry's desk, braiding her hair into her familiar pigtails. She had taken off Sabrina's clothes and was now wearing a pair of cotton candy–colored pajamas with little stars on them. Her face was cleanly scrubbed of the lip gloss, and she had folded Sabrina's clothes neatly and set them on the bed.

"Are you OK?" Sabrina said.

"We don't have to talk about it, Sabrina," the little girl said. "In fact, I'd rather not."

Sabrina was taken back by her sister's attitude. "You're angry about the weapon. Well, I can explain—"

"I don't want to talk about it," Daphne interrupted.

"Well, I think we should. I want to explain my side of what happened."

Daphne burst into tears. "How are you going to explain that you stole from me, kept a secret, and lied about it? How are you going to explain that you . . . that you betrayed me?"

"You don't even know what *betrayed* means!"

"Yes, I do!" Daphne said, heaving a new paperback dictionary at her sister. "I looked it up."

Sabrina bent down and picked up her sister's dictionary. "Yes, I lied to you. I stole the key and snuck out and took the weapon without you knowing. You were too young to have that kind of responsibility and you refused to see the danger we are in, so I did it."

"You treat me like I'm a baby, Sabrina. I'm not a baby!"

"I have a reason to be angry, too! You've been walking around here for days, wearing my clothes, mocking me. I've seen you roll your eyes and your snarky comments. You think it's nice to be made fun of?"

"I wasn't making fun of you, Sabrina. I was trying to be more like you. You're my role model," Daphne said. "I was dressing like you and wearing my hair like yours 'cause I was trying to grow up a little. I wanted to be more like my sister. But not anymore."

Sabrina looked at the stack of clothing on the bed.

"I think I'll go back to being myself. I like me," Daphne said.

Sabrina searched for words, but they were jumbled like pieces of a jigsaw puzzle that didn't fit together.

"I wasn't making fun of you. I love you. Though, I don't like you very much," the little girl said. "And it's obvious to me that you don't like me much, either."

"That's not true!" Sabrina said.

"I'm not going to bother you anymore. I'm sleeping in Granny's room tonight. Tomorrow, Mr. Boarman and Mr. Swineheart are going to come over and build me my own bedroom," her sister said. She finished with her hair and got up from the desk. "Hand it over."

Sabrina shuffled her feet. "What, the kazoo?"

"You can't handle it. It's magic, Sabrina. Give it to me."

"But—"

Daphne shook her head. "Don't argue with me. Just hand it over."

Sabrina dug into her pocket for the kazoo. Her fingers tingled when she touched it. It made her feel good, but she knew that feeling was false. She knew her sister was right. She took it out of her pocket and handed it to Daphne.

"I have something of yours," the little girl said, digging into her overalls. She pulled a tube of lip gloss out of her pocket and placed it into Sabrina's hand; then she walked into the hallway and closed the door behind her.

Sabrina bit her lip so hard she tasted blood. She wanted to cry but couldn't anymore. Puck had been right. He had warned her that the truth would come out and when it did, it would be ugly. That's the only thing he got wrong—it wasn't just ugly, it was horrible.

• • •

The next morning, Robin and Little John arrived bright and early.

"We've got some bad news," Little John said when Granny asked them in.

"The tape is missing," Robin explained. "Everything Hatchett said is gone. We've got no evidence!"

"What happened?" Sabrina cried.

"We don't know, but we have our suspicions," Robin said. "You know that snail on the jury, the one with the Scarlet Hand mark on his chest?"

"Sure!" Daphne said.

"Well, this morning when I woke up the tape was gone, and there was a trail of slime leading to the front door. The place smelled like apple tobacco, too."

"We don't have a lot of hope if the jury is trying to sabotage our case," Little John replied.

"Worse still, Bluebeard is calling Red Riding Hood to the stand today. I'm sure she'll back up Hatchett's story," Robin said.

"Maybe not," Daphne said as she removed the kazoo from her pocket. "I have an idea that might put a whammy into Bluebeard's case."

"A whammy?" Robin Hood asked.

"It's my new word. It means something no one saw coming."

Little John scooped Daphne up into his arms. "Well, young lady. We could really use a whammy right about now!"

• • •

Nurse Sprat seemed startled when the group returned to the hospital. She nearly choked on her pork chop sandwich.

"You want to see her again? No one ever wants to see her again."

She led the group down the familiar hallway and unlocked Red's door. The child was sitting at the same little table having the same tea party she had had the last time they had visited. Sabrina wondered if Red had even gone to bed. Before Sprat could lock them in, Sabrina turned to her.

"Would you happen to have an empty jar with a tight lid?"

"Why?" Sprat asked.

"Let's just say it's going to make your job here at the hospital a lot easier."

Sprat shrugged. "I'll check," she said, then locked the door.

"You came back," Red said, clapping her hands. "Please, sit, have some tea!"

Daphne sat down at the table. "I'd love some," Daphne said, as she took the kazoo from her pocket.

Sabrina stood behind her. "Red, do you remember when we said you were sick inside your brain?"

Red nodded.

"Well, how would you like to feel better?"

Red clapped. "Then I can go home."

Robin joined the girls at the table. "Girls, I'm worried about this. Daphne has never tried to use this kazoo before. If what you say is true, it can demolish a house with one little puff."

"I've used it a couple of times. It kind of does what you want it to," Sabrina explained.

"Except for the time you destroyed the bank," Puck reminded her.

"OK, about fifty percent of the time it works like a charm."

"I'm still a bit confused," Little John said. "Are you planning to blow this crazy child into the next county? What good will that do us?"

"It does more than blow houses down. Right, Daphne?" Sabrina said. The little girl nodded. "It cures the mentally insane."

"Uh, maybe you should turn it on yourself, 'cause you sound crazy," Puck replied.

Sabrina was about to roll her eyes but she caught herself. She looked to Daphne for permission to continue explaining. The little girl nodded again. "Let me start from the very beginning. We know from the story of Red Riding Hood that her mother sent her into the forest with a basket of food to deliver to her grandmother. That part of the story has always been a little odd. Who sends a child into the woods where wild animals live? That is not good parenting."

"Good point," Uncle Jake said.

"We think Mr. Hatchett told us the reason, though I doubt he meant to. The truth is Red's family was at their wit's end with her. They were desperate. They sent her to the grandmother's because they were hoping she could do something to help her."

"My mommy and daddy love me," Red said.

"They wanted you to get better," Sabrina said to the girl. Red nodded and hugged a stuffed doll with a missing head.

"Hatchett says Red's granny was a witch, and when he showed up she was blowing a little flute that could manipulate the wind. Well, he got it wrong. It wasn't a flute. It was a kazoo."

Daphne held it up for everyone to see. Sabrina continued, "Red's grandmother either found the kazoo or created it herself. From Hatchett's version, it could control the wind. But we think it does more than that. The kazoo creates a wind that literally blows the insanity out of a person. When Hatchett and Canis stumbled upon the grandmother's house, they watched the witch blow the madness out of a rabid wolf. She bottled it up but she wasn't doing this to heal a sick animal. She was testing the kazoo to make sure it worked before she tried it on her granddaughter."

"She was trying to fix Red," Granny marveled.

Sabrina nodded. "At least we think she was. Mr. Canis, or Tobias Clay, or whatever his name was, just got in the way. He was trying to be a hero and save Red. He is the real hero wood-cutter from the story, not Howard Hatchett."

"And you want to try this on Red? Hatchett told us it was dangerous. The madness from the rabid wolf merged with Mr. Canis to become the Big Bad Wolf," Uncle Jake said. "What happens if Red's madness slips into one of us? The Wolf part of Canis is completely insane. Canis has never been able to fully control it."

"We have to be careful," Sabrina said. There was a knock at the door and when the locks were all undone it swung open. Nurse Sprat held a glass jar in her nervous hands.

"Here!" she cried, then shoved it into Sabrina's hands and slammed the door tight.

"This jar will do the trick, I hope," Sabrina said. "If the three pigs had had a jar when they beat the Wolf and took the kazoo from him, we might have been rid of the monster for good, but they had no idea what the kazoo was capable of. They just thought it was how the Wolf huffed and puffed his way around town. But when they turned it on him, the Wolf was gone and Canis was left behind. The rabid wolf's insanity left Canis, allowing him to take control of his body, even when the insanity swirled back into him. But as we've been seeing, he wasn't that much in control, and he's slowly changing back."

"So if we can trap Red's insanity in a jar, then she can tell what she remembers from that day?" Robin asked.

Sabrina nodded. "The only chance of saving Canis is if an Everafter stands up for him. If we fix Red, she can do that for us."

"It doesn't hurt that she's in the Scarlet Hand," Uncle Jake added.

"Should I do it now?" Daphne asked.

"Yes. When I turned it on the Black Knight, I concentrated on having the power affect him only. I think the wind will do what you ask it to," Sabrina encouraged her sister.

Daphne raised the kazoo to her lips and blew. The wind blasted out of it, upending the dolls, tea set, and anything else that wasn't nailed down. The people, however, seemed unfazed, except for their hair flying around.

Red Riding Hood glanced around her and started to laugh. "Bad weather!" she shrieked. "Very bad weather."

The wind swirled around her like a snake. It crept around every limb, embraced her tightly, and then pulled back. Red cried out in pain as the group watched something horrible and black seep out of her. To call it a person would be wrong. It was more like an animal, with fangs and with eyes like bottomless pits. To Sabrina, it looked like some horribly mutated worm seeking revenge on a fisherman. It whipped around in midair,

desperate to reach Red Riding Hood, but the wind kept it at bay. It shrieked angrily.

"Now, Sabrina!" Granny cried.

Sabrina opened the glass jar and reached out to the creature. It thrashed about as Daphne forced it into the jar. Once it was inside, Sabrina quickly tightened the lid and the wind vanished. She watched her sister look at the little kazoo and slip it back into her pocket. Then she turned to Red Riding Hood. The strange girl had collapsed to the ground and lay still.

"She's hurt," Robin Hood said, as he rushed to her side, but his concerns proved to be unwarranted. Red opened her eyes slowly and looked up into the face of Granny Relda.

"Grandmother?" she asked.

Sabrina's heart sank. She had been wrong. She believed they could really heal the girl, and that she in turn could save Mr. Canis, but Red was just as crazy as before. The weapon had not done what she had hoped it would.

The door to the room flew open and slammed against the wall. Sabrina looked up and saw Bluebeard and Nottingham barging into the room, along with half a dozen card soldiers armed with swords.

"Sorry, Grimms!" Nottingham said. "We have to take our witness to the trial."

One of the card soldiers dragged Red to her feet and pulled her from the room.

"I do hope you had enough time to question her," Bluebeard said. "Though I suspect you didn't get too many straight answers out of her."

Nottingham and Bluebeard roared with laughter as they left the room.

"See you in court," Bluebeard cried back over his shoulder. "The trial starts in fifteen minutes."

• • •

The family rushed to the courthouse and pushed their way through the crowd at the entrance. There were no seats left and they were forced to stand in the back of the room.

Mayor Heart made her way over to the family. She had a wicked grin on her face. Her crooked yellow teeth made Sabrina's stomach turn more than her mean-spirited comments. "Looks like today's the day we wrap this all up, Grimms. I suspect your Wolf will meet the nooseman by this time tomorrow."

Granny frowned as the woman walked away. "Isn't she a delight?"

Judge Hatter entered the courtroom and made his way to the front where his desk once stood. Since he had smashed it with a sledgehammer the day before, it had been replaced with a stack of milk crates. He didn't seem to notice. The Four of Spades called for order and announced the judge as he sat down.

"Let's get started," Judge Hatter said. "We can't exactly get ended can we? No, I suppose we can't. Can we? Or is it, may we? We may. No, we may not. Mr. Bluebeard, do you have a new witness?"

Bluebeard stood up from his desk and surveyed the crowd. He had a smug look on his face and he beamed at everyone, including Sabrina and her family. "Indeed I do. In fact, she's our last witness. I call Little Red Riding Hood to the stand."

The crowd fell silent as if their words were forcefully stuffed back into their mouths. The double doors in the back opened and a card soldier escorted Red to the stand. He helped her into her seat and stood nearby, watching her closely.

"Does the witness need to be watched?" Hatter asked.

The card soldier nodded. "This one is especially dangerous. She's mentally deranged, sir."

"Oh," Hatter said with delight. "How exciting! What does she do? Eat people? Push people out of windows? Throw knives?"

"All of the above, I believe."

The judge clapped like a happy child. "It's nice to not feel so alone. Bluebeard, ask your questions."

The lawyer approached the little girl, but even he kept a safe distance from her. When she looked up into his face he smiled, but she sat there, stone-faced and gazing around as if lost in thought.

"Precious girl," Bluebeard started. "You have been through so much. I hate to put you through any more but we need to get to the truth. We have a . . . ahem . . . man on trial for his life, so I hope you'll be brave and answer some questions."

Red continued gazing about. Sabrina had seen this expression before. The little lunatic was probably having another delusion.

"Red, we've already established that your parents sent you to see your grandmother and asked you to take a basket of food and medicine. Do you know why they sent you?"

"Momma told me Granny was sick," Red said.

"Your grandmother was sick? How sad. So you went through the woods following a path to her house. When you got there, what did you see?"

"A monster," Red said.

Bluebeard smiled. "Can you point out that monster?"

Without as much as a glance, Red pointed at Mr. Canis.

"Let the record show that the child pointed at the accused," the lawyer said, then turned his attention back to Red. "Where was your grandmother when you arrived?"

"The Wolf ate her," Red said softly.

"That's terrible," Bluebeard said overdramatically. He looked as if he might burst into tears, but Sabrina knew he was acting. "I'm sure you know this, but the story of what happened has been spread far and wide. In one version you came into the house and found the Wolf hiding in your grandmother's bed. Is that what happened?"

Red nodded.

"Why would he do that?" Bluebeard asked.

"He wanted to trick me so he could eat me, too," Red said.

"Luckily, a woodcutter came and saved your life," Bluebeard said as he turned to the jury. His face was pure confidence.

"No, that's not what happened."

Bluebeard's face fell. He spun around to face Red once more. "I'm sorry, child. Maybe you misunderstood what I said. I was talking about the brave woodcutter who saved your life."

Red shook her head. "I heard what you said. I said that isn't what happened. I found the woodcutter hiding in the fields."

"Then how did you escape the Wolf?" Bluebeard asked.

"Because he saved me from himself," Red said, pointing at Mr. Canis.

The crowd broke into excited chatter. Hatter pounded a gavel down on the stack of milk crates. They collapsed before him.

With nothing to pound on, he slammed the gavel into his own head. "Order!"

"The jury should be careful about what the witness says. She's mentally ill," Bluebeard said.

"Objection!" Robin Hood cried. "If her testimony can't be trusted then why is she here? She's either telling the whole truth or telling a whole lie."

"Order!" Hatter demanded, slamming his head against a wall. "Mr. Bluebeard, do you have any more questions?"

Bluebeard looked frantic. "No, sir!"

Judge Hatter, however, had some of his own. "You say the creature who murdered your grandmother saved your life?"

Red nodded. "My grandmother was trying to heal me. I've struggled with my sanity since I was a baby. She was a witch, and she had a plan, but it blew up around her. The result was she created the Big Bad Wolf, and that poor man, the one they call Mr. Canis, was the real victim. He was in the wrong place at the wrong time. He didn't mean to kill my grandmother but he couldn't stop himself. Lucky for me, he got control over himself for a brief moment and begged me to run."

"You say you've dealt with your sanity for a long time," Hatter said. "I know crazy and you seem perfectly fine to me."

Red scanned the crowd and found Sabrina and her family. She smiled. "I'm feeling much better."

"Objection!" Bluebeard cried. "We are finished with this witness."

Judge Hatter snarled at Bluebeard. "I say when a witness is ready to go."

"It's true that the Wolf killed my grandma, but I don't think he could control himself. He was out of his mind. I know how that feels. I've done terrible things. I know it. The Wolf is dangerous but he does not deserve to die."

"Objection!" Mayor Heart roared from her seat.

"Your honor. We rest our case," Bluebeard said, frantically. "We'd like the jury to make its decision."

Hatter shrugged. "Fine with me. We'll take a one-hour break to allow the jury to decide."

"So we don't get to question this witness, either?" Robin Hood shouted.

"Objection!" Hatter shouted.

"I beg your pardon," said the bewildered lawyer.

"I object," the judge replied.

"You're the judge. You don't get to object," Robin cried.

"Well I object to not being allowed to object. I find it . . . objectionable," Hatter replied. "The court finds the Wolf not guilty!" he slammed his head with the gavel and then prepared to leave.

"Your honor!" Bluebeard cried. "The jury has to vote on whether the Wolf is guilty. You can't do that yourself."

"Oh, another of your silly rules," the judge said. "Very well, I declare a recess. One hour."

Judge Hatter got off his chair and raced through the aisle toward the double doors. Sabrina watched him pass, marveling at the fact that his neck could support his monstrous head and nose. As soon as he left, the crowd surged out behind him.

• • •

The family congregated at Briar Rose's coffee shop. Briar took a break and sat with them, but not before she brought everyone fresh muffins and steaming cups of coffee. Sabrina, Puck, and Daphne were treated to chocolate milk with whipped cream on top. The princess sat next to Uncle Jake and kissed him on the cheek. Sabrina watched Briar's fairy godmothers stew with anger.

"They're going to turn me into a frog," Uncle Jake said, grinning.

"Well, I won't be the first princess in this town to date an amphibian," Briar said.

"What do you think Canis's chances are?" Uncle Jake asked Granny.

The old woman sipped her coffee. "Who can say? The Judge is pretty unpredictable."

"The judge is a certifiable nutbag," Puck said.

Granny nodded. "But he doesn't seem to be in Mayor Heart's pocket, either. I think they thought that having an insane person as the judge might sway things in their favor. I don't think it's turning out that way. He's proving to be unpredictable for us all."

"Maybe too unpredictable," Sabrina said.

"I think Judge Hatter is the Scarlet Hand's whammy," Daphne said as she brushed whipped cream off her nose.

Just then, one of Robin Hood's merry men came running into the coffee shop. He was out of breath and so excited he could barely speak.

"The . . . jury . . . is . . . back," he gasped.

Everyone jumped up from their seats and followed the lawyer at a run until they got back to the courtroom. The double doors were closed and two card soldiers blocked the way.

"Court is in session. No one can enter," the Eight of Diamonds said.

"You let me in right now, or I swear the two of you will get the shuffling of your life," Granny said.

Befuddled, the guards stepped aside and Granny threw the

doors open. Every person in the packed courtroom turned to gape at the noisy newcomers.

"Uhm, as I was saying," Judge Hatter said. "Has the jury reached a verdict?"

The man in the black cloak stood up from his seat. He held a folded piece of paper in his hands. "We have," he said. There was something familiar about his voice, but Sabrina couldn't place it.

"Very good. Read your verdict," Hatter replied.

The man cleared his throat and unfolded the paper. "We the jury find the accused guilty of murder."

Sabrina gasped. Most of the audience cheered, though Sabrina heard some angry boos coming from their loyal friends. The noise banged against Sabrina's eardrums like a wooden spoon on an old pot. She felt dizzy and sick to her stomach. Granny and Daphne looked no better.

"I see," Hatter said when the crowd grew quiet. "Then I suppose we need to sentence him, and I tell you folks, I'm going to give him a full sentence. Not a sentence fragment but a whole sentence with a verb and a noun and possibly an adjective. I wouldn't be surprised if there was a conjunction in there as well. I can't stand these judges who run around with their half-baked sentences. That's how you get salmonella poisoning! Thus, I sentence the Wolf to death by hanging!"

The crowd leaped to its feet. Some were dancing and clapping; others laughed and howled with twisted joy. Only Sabrina, her family, Briar Rose, Snow White, and their Everafter friends were brokenhearted.

"Order! Order in the court!" Hatter cried, striking his head with his gavel again. "The Wolf will be hanged tomorrow in the center of town at noon. I believe we should make an example out of the monster. This case is over!"

Hatter leaped to his feet and rushed out of the room. Bluebeard, however, stood beaming proudly at the Grimms. Robin Hood and Little John pushed through the crowd to them. Their long faces spoke a thousand words of remorse. Granny thanked them for trying then moved to the front of the court where Mr. Canis was being dragged away by a dozen soldiers.

"Old friend!" she said.

"Old friend," Canis said, his features now almost completely those of the Wolf's.

"We'll work on another way," Granny said. "There's no reason to worry."

Canis shook his head. "It's over, Relda Grimm. It is how I want it."

He turned and allowed the guards to lead him out of the courtroom.

Daphne hugged her grandmother and wept into the old woman's dress. Tears were rolling down Granny's face as well. Even Uncle Jake was shaken and pale. Puck, however, was furious.

"I'm going to rescue him!" he shouted angrily. His wings sprang from his back and his eyes turned coal black. He snatched his sword from his waist and flew toward the door that Canis had been led through, but Granny pulled him back by his foot.

"No, Puck!"

"He needs our help, old lady!" Puck shouted.

"No! Not here. Not this way. If you go after him they will arrest you next. Stay with us, Puck. I can't bear to lose another member of my family."

"What now?" Sabrina asked her grandmother. For the first time since she had met the old woman, her granny was speechless. She seemed dumbstruck by something at the far end of the room. Sabrina followed her gaze and saw the man in the black cloak staring back at them. Bluebeard joined him and shook his hand, as did Heart and Nottingham. And then something so much more shocking occurred than even Canis's death sentence. The man reached up and removed his hood, revealing his identity. The man in the cloak was Prince William Charming.

Snow White saw the unveiling as well. Her already pale complexion grew whiter. She bit her lower lip and a tear rolled down her cheek. She turned to Granny Relda. "I'm sorry," she whispered. "I can't be here."

Snow turned and ran out of the room. Charming watched her go, but then turned back to his new friends. Sabrina glared at the man like he was mold on the bottom of a toilet. She had never trusted Charming, but she had secretly hoped that Daphne was right about him. The little girl always believed he was a hero waiting for an opportunity. Even though he had come to the family's aid occasionally, Sabrina had continued to have her doubts. It had never felt so miserable to be so right.

10

n the day the Big Bad Wolf was sentenced to die, it rained. Buckets of water spilled from dull, black clouds and flooded the streets. The town's sewer system backed up and the water that didn't make it to the nearby river flowed through the tiny hamlet without restraint.

Granny Relda wrapped herself in a rain jacket. Uncle Jake stood beside her holding an umbrella over her head. Sabrina recognized it as the same umbrella Mr. Canis had held over her the day she and Daphne arrived in Ferryport Landing. At first the children were told they had to stay home. Then Granny seemed to realize they'd sneak out anyway, and so she agreed to let them come along to say good-bye, but they were not to watch the execution. Sabrina knew it might be the last chance she had to apologize to the man who had been her family's protector for almost two decades. She wanted to tell him how wrong she had been about him. He had never deserved her distrust.

The family drove to Main Street in their old jalopy. Sabrina sat remembering the times she had had with Canis. For the first time, the chaos and noise of the car went unnoticed.

They parked on a side street and walked up the block. In the center of Main Street, a large platform had been constructed. It had two levels. One was wide and close to the ground, the second was at the top of a tower, high above the other. A wooden beam held a noose above the second platform. A huge crowd had already gathered. Sabrina and her family moved to the front. Along the way, Everafters shouted angry comments and filthy words at them: The Grimms were a blight and a menace. They were disgusting and filthy humans. They were inferior and stupid and the cause of everyone's suffering.

Bluebeard, Nottingham, Mayor Heart, and Charming appeared on the first platform. The crowd cheered their arrival and Heart waved like she was in a beauty pageant.

"We've waited a long time for this, haven't we?" she shouted into her megaphone. Many in the crowd roared back at her. Most wore the mark of the Scarlet Hand. Heart raised her hand for their attention, then turned her gaze on the family. "But trust me, people. Today is just the beginning. Bring out the Wolf!"

The crowd cheered and broke into a chant of "Bring out the Wolf!"

Half a dozen card soldiers appeared with Canis in their midst. He towered over them, but they had swords, and Canis did not look as if he was going to put up a fight. The guards pushed him up to the second tower and the Ace of Spades wrapped a noose around his thick, hairy neck.

"I'd like to speak to my friend," Granny said. She pushed her way to the tower and climbed the stairs.

"You'll be up there yourself, soon!" someone shouted from the crowd.

Sabrina watched her grandmother talk to Canis. She couldn't hear what she was saying, but it was obvious to her that Granny was begging him to break free and escape. He shook his head and spoke to her softly.

"What is she doing?" a voice said from behind them. Sabrina turned and found Snow White.

"I think she's trying to convince him to make a run for it and kill anyone who gets in his way," Uncle Jake said.

"He doesn't seem to be listening," Snow said.

"That's because he's smart," another voice said. This one belonged to Bluebeard, who was standing uncomfortably close to the beautiful teacher. "Personally, I think he's welcoming the opportunity to end his suffering. He's committed so many atrocities. It must be hard on his soul."

"You would know," Snow said.

Bluebeard's face turned crimson, but he calmed himself and even laughed. "Indeed."

Sabrina couldn't stand to be near him any longer. She snatched her sister's hand, and together they climbed the tower to Granny and Canis.

"Girls, it's not safe," the old woman said.

"I need to say good-bye," Sabrina said.

"Me, too," Daphne added.

"I have been very rude to you. I have never treated you with the respect you deserved," Sabrina said to Canis, then she turned to her sister. "It's a problem I have. I seem to treat everyone badly."

"You are young, Sabrina Grimm," Canis said. "Time will supply you with wisdom. I'm sorry I will not be around to see how you use it."

Daphne clung to Canis and hugged him tightly. "Good-bye, Tobias Clay."

Canis looked confused.

"That was your name, before. You were a man once, free of the monster," Sabrina said.

Canis shook his head. "A man? Is that true? I don't remember anything before the incident. Did I have a wife? Children? Who was I?"

"We don't know," Sabrina said.

Mr. Canis seemed shocked. "If only I had known this—"

"Get your children down, now!" Heart bellowed through her megaphone.

Granny said a final good-bye and ushered the girls down the steps. They were only halfway down when Heart began shouting again.

"Does the prisoner have any final words?"

Canis looked out at the crowd and laughed.

"What's so funny, mongrel?" Heart shouted.

"Look at all the monsters," he said.

Heart snarled and pulled a lever. The floor beneath Canis slid open and his body fell like a stone. Sabrina knew that looking would haunt her for the rest of her life, but she couldn't help herself. But Canis was not swinging from the end of a rope. In fact, he had landed on his feet on the ground. The rope was sliced in two and a red-quilled arrow was buried in the ground behind the platform. The crowd gasped and turned their attention away from the gallows. There, standing across the street, was Robin Hood, no longer in his suit and tie, but in a green shirt and brown tights. He was holding a bow with a second arrow trained on Mayor Heart. Little John stood next to him with a long wooden staff. Will Scarlet,

Friar Tuck, and the rest of the Merry Men stood behind them.

"We're back," Little John bellowed with a grin. "Did you miss us?"

Robin Hood waved to the crowd. "For those of you wondering, the Sherwood Group is officially closed for business. Don't worry about us, we'll find other jobs. You know what they say, 'do what you love and the money will come.' I look forward to robbing all of you in the very near future."

"That guy is so cool," Puck said.

Nottingham pulled his sword. "I'll kill you, Robin. This time I'll make sure of it." He dashed into the crowd, pushing and shoving in his eagerness to get to Robin.

The Merry Men rushed into the crowd as well, turning it into an enormous mob. Everyone was fighting—members of the Scarlet Hand even fought one another. Uncle Jake pulled Briar to safety. Then he found Granny and the girls and did the same. Puck, however, flew over the crowd, smacking the tops of people's heads with his wooden sword.

"We have to get out of here," Uncle Jake said, reaching into his pockets to arm himself with magical items.

"What about Mr. Canis?" Daphne asked.

Sabrina could see the huge man tossing people aside and roaring. "I think he's OK."

"Are we all here?" Granny asked.

Sabrina scanned the crowd. "Where's Ms. White?"

In the chaos it was obvious that even a trained self-defense teacher like Snow could be seriously injured. Sabrina shouted at Puck. "Hey, dirtface. Find Snow White!"

Puck nodded and zipped away. A moment later he was back. "I found her. She's in trouble. Follow me!"

The family raced after the flying boy. He took them a block away and down an alley. There they found Ms. White being dragged away by Bluebeard.

"Leave her alone!" Daphne shouted as they approached.

Bluebeard sneered. "You people run along. Snow and I are going to have a little talk about manners."

Snow punched him in the face and he fell backward, but he sprang back to his feet almost immediately. He wrapped his arm around her neck and pulled a dagger from his pocket. He ran the tip along Snow's throat.

"Stand back, folks. Let's not get excited. I'd hate for someone to lose their head," Bluebeard said. "Snow and I need to come to an understanding. I am a patient man but my patience has worn thin. I asked you out for a date and you rejected me. Do you know how that hurts?"

"You disgust me!" Snow cried.

"See what I mean? That's just rude. I'm a very nice man, a pure gentleman, who wanted to take you out for dinner, and this is how you treat me."

Sabrina heard someone running toward them. She spun around to find Charming approaching from the main street.

"Billy!" Snow cried.

"Charming," Bluebeard said. "Have they captured the Wolf yet?"

"No, not yet," Charming said.

"I was just having a conversation with Snow about how to respect other people," Bluebeard said.

"I see. How is it going?"

"Not well. I wanted to give your ex a chance to redeem herself. She's no friend of the Hand, what with her relationship with these lousy Grimms. I had hoped that if she were to get involved with me, it might save her life when the Master rises."

"It's hopeless," Charming said. "I've tried."

"Billy, what are you saying?" Snow cried.

Charming approached them and stared Snow hard in the face. "You've got yourself into another situation, Snow."

"William, you don't mind if I have a little fun with her?" Bluebeard asked. "If you're done with her like you say you are, then you won't mind."

Charming was still, then he nodded.

He turned to walk back to the riot, but in a flash there was a

sword in his hand. He whipped around and plunged it into Blue-beard's side. The villain collapsed with the blade still in him. Snow broke free of his grasp and stumbled away. Bluebeard reached out for her, but then his eyes closed and he was still.

"I didn't see that one coming," Puck whispered to Sabrina.

Snow was trembling when Charming pulled her to his side. "You hate me," he said. "I get that. And I would apologize, but I can't. I did all of this—the betrayal, the cruelty, joining this wretched Hand—I did it all to save your life."

Charming released her and turned to Granny. "Canis has fled."

"What? Where did he go?"

"Robin told him about Hatchett. Canis was furious and he ran off," he said. "Relda, he was injured and something inside snapped. I think the Wolf is finally in charge."

"Mom, if the Wolf gets to Hatchett before we do, he'll kill him," Uncle Jake said.

Granny took Daphne's hand. "Do you still have that kazoo?" The little girl nodded.

"It might be our only chance."

• • •

A caravan of cars raced through the twisting country roads of Ferryport Landing. In the first, there was Sabrina, Puck, and Daphne in the back, with Granny, Uncle Jake, and Briar Rose squeezed into the front. The second was driven by Snow White with Prince Charming in the passenger seat; Little John and his wooden staff took up the backseat. The third car held the rest of the Merry Men.

Uncle Jake pushed the family car to the limit. Driving around the block was more than the old car should have been able to take, but Jake managed to get the vehicle over the speed limit. Small flickers of flame flashed from under the hood. Sabrina tried not to notice. She suspected her uncle and grandmother were doing the same.

Next to her Daphne held the kazoo. She turned it over and over, studying every part of it. Daphne caught her staring and mouthed that she was preparing herself. No one could have a conversation in the noisy car.

Soon they found the entrance to Hatchettland. Uncle Jake slid into an empty parking spot and turned off the ignition. Everyone leaped out and gathered together.

"Do you think we beat him here?" Robin asked.

Somewhere down the path, Hatchett screamed and there was a terrible roar.

"I wouldn't bet money on it," Puck said as he freed his sword. Then he turned and raced down the path. Everyone followed until they came to the ancient house. Once there, Sabrina could see the door had been ripped off its hinges and tossed aside.

"Children, you are to keep your distance from Mr. Canis," Granny said.

"I came here to fight," Puck complained.

Granny ignored him. She turned to Daphne and smiled.

"Are you ready?"

Daphne held up the kazoo and nodded.

Granny turned to the house and called out to Mr. Canis. There was no response, so she called out to the Wolf. A moment later, the hulking creature stomped through the doorway. He dragged a kicking and screaming Hatchett behind him.

"Well, well, well," the Wolf said. "If it isn't everyone's favorite family, the Grimms. And look, you've brought friends. Good, I'm famished."

"Let Hatchett go," Granny begged.

The Wolf laughed. "Relda, you really do make me laugh. You truly don't understand me. I am a beast and I must do beastly things. You tried to help Canis keep me locked up. But I'm free now, no longer bound by the old man's chains. I'm back in action and I'm eager to spill some blood."

"I know that Mr. Canis is still in there," Granny said.

The Wolf chuckled. "You're right, Relda. If only you'd come closer, reach out to me, take my hand, maybe you could coax him out. Come on, give it a try. See what happens."

"Let the man go!" Robin Hood shouted. He had an arrow trained on the Wolf.

Hatchett squealed and begged for someone to save him.

"Can you believe this guy? He built this place to honor his bravery," the Wolf said. "The brave hero who destroyed me is sobbing like a baby."

"Wolf, I'm going to give you one last chance to stop this now," Granny said, sternly.

The Wolf raised his eyebrows in surprise. "Relda, you're threatening me!"

"I'm serious."

"We should talk about this," the Wolf said, looking at Howard Hatchett. "Just let me finish my lunch." He opened his jaws wide and bit down hard on Hatchett's arm. The man cried out in agony.

"Daphne, do it," Granny said, as she stepped aside. Daphne placed the kazoo in her mouth and blew a long, fuzzy note. The wind appeared from nowhere, blasting through the surrounding trees and sending leaves and branches flying in all directions. The Wolf released Hatchett and glared at the little girl.

"That belongs to me!" he growled and leaped forward. He was nearly on top of Daphne when Robin's arrow sank into the Wolf's arm. He howled in pain and pulled it out. He continued toward the little girl but was knocked to his knees when Little John pounded him on the back with his staff. Puck leaped into the air and landed on the Wolf's shoulders, standing. With his sword he smacked the beast on the top of its head, and then he backflipped out of the way. None of this had much effect on the monster, and the beast lunged forward once again.

This time the Wolf pinned Daphne to the ground. The little girl kept blowing into the kazoo, but the desired effect was either not working or taking too long. All Sabrina could think to do was jump on the Wolf's back. She punched and kicked, driving her limbs into the monster's tough hide with all she had. She could hear him laughing, maybe at her efforts but maybe also at the fear in Daphne's face. He opened his mouth and revealed his horrid teeth and prepared to sink them into Sabrina's sister when the wind wrapped around him. It was almost visible, the snakelike clinging. Once it was tightly around the monster it began to pull.

The Wolf snarled and struggled as if he had gotten caught in a hunter's trap. He cursed Daphne, bellowed threats, swore he'd tear her limb from limb, but the wind prevented him from harming her. Sabrina, too, was helpless in the blustery cage. She did her best to let go of the Wolf but she was firmly locked in the wind's grip. And then the writhing shadow creature was pulled out of Canis. Like Red Riding Hood's, it was horrible, but this one was more the shape of a wolf, snapping and spitting, with foam dripping from its jaws. It hovered above them, howling and screaming, helpless in the magic of the wind. Sabrina looked down and realized that she was no longer clinging to the Wolf. Lying on the ground beneath her was Mr. Canis. He was unconscious but breathing.

"Sabrina, try to break free," Granny cried, but nothing Sabrina did seemed to help. All she could do was look into the shadow creature's terrible eyes. It howled in her face, and then she felt an odd sensation, as if the wind had blown through her, like it had seeped into her skin. The wind disappeared and all was calm. She looked around for the monster, hoping someone had captured it.

"Where did it go?" she said, though her voice sounded odd, deep and scratchy. But the rest of her body felt wonderful—strong and fast and unstoppable. In fact, Sabrina had never felt as confident as she did at that moment. For the first time in a long time she wasn't worried about monsters, villains, or lunatics. She didn't fear surprise attacks or betrayal by people she trusted. In fact, she was eager for a confrontation.

She wanted to share the feeling with her sister but the words were hard to find. Her thoughts were cloudy and complicated. She tried to say something but it came out sounding like a horrible, hungry laugh. She turned to Daphne. The little girl was undergoing her own transformation. A swirling black fog circled her body, blocking out most of her face. All Sabrina could see were the little girl's eyes, like two brilliant suns.

"Sabrina, you have to stop this!" Granny cried.

Sabrina was confused. What did the old woman mean? She wasn't doing anything wrong.

"Sabrina, please! Don't make me do this to you," Daphne begged from behind the black fog.

"What are you talking about?" Sabrina said, noticing the shiny toy in her sister's hand.

"You have to fight this!" Daphne said. "I know you are still in there. Don't let him control you!"

"Have you lost your mind? Why are you talking to me like this?" Sabrina asked. When no one replied, she realized that her words were only in her head.

"Fight him, child," a voice said from below, and Sabrina glanced down. Mr. Canis lay at her feet—old and withered, his body trapped in the clutches of a huge, fur-covered paw. It was squeezing the life from the old man's chest. She cried out, hoping someone would help her pull her friend from its terrible grip, but her cries ceased when she realized the claws that were killing Mr. Canis were her own.

She had become the Big Bad Wolf.

She stomped into the house and found a dingy mirror on the wall. One look sent her into shock. Her whole body had been transformed. Her long blond hair was gone, replaced by thick, matted fur that covered her entire body. Her hands were huge and the fingers curled into horrible claws. She spun around and found a bushy tail behind her. It was insanity! How could this have happened? She roared angrily and then smashed the mirror in front of her.

"I'll fix this," Daphne said from behind her. Sabrina turned to look at the little girl, unsure of who she was or what she wanted. Seeing her made Sabrina hungry. She imagined grabbing the girl and—no—she knew she had to fight her impulse but how could she? Her need, her hunger, was overwhelming.

And then the wind returned and everything went black.

• • •

When Sabrina awoke she was back to her normal self. She lay in the bed in the little wooden house that Red Riding Hood's grandmother had slept in hundreds of years before. Standing near her was her family. Daphne was crying and wiping the tears on her sleeve. Mr. Canis was there, too. In his hand he held a glass mason jar. Inside, Sabrina could see a dark, black creature desperate to escape. Briar, Snow, and Charming were there, as well as Robin and Little John and the rest of the Merry Men.

"How are you feeling, child?" Canis asked.

"Normal," Sabrina said, examining her arms to make sure they were free of fur.

Canis chuckled. "It's a wonderful feeling."

"Is it over?" she asked him.

He nodded. "In a manner of speaking."

Granny Relda bent down and felt her forehead.

"You've had quite a day," the old woman said as the air filled with sirens.

"Here comes Nottingham," Robin said. "So are we decided?"

Charming and Canis looked one another in the eye and then shook hands. "Yes," they said.

"What's going on?" Sabrina said. Charming and Canis were usually bitter enemies.

"I'm afraid that—after you and your family—we've become Ferryport Landing's most wanted," Charming said.

"Right where we belong," Little John bellowed.

Canis smiled slightly. "We're going to have to hide out for a while."

"There are places in the mountains where no one will find us," Snow said.

"You're going, too?" Sabrina asked the teacher.

Snow nodded, then turned to Charming. "Someone has to look after this bunch of troublemakers."

"I won't be far," Canis said to Granny.

"I know, old friend."

One of the Merry Men raced into the room. "They're coming down the path."

Canis finally turned to Puck. "You're in charge, boy."

"Haven't I always been?" Puck said.

"Then we're off," Robin said. "Don't worry, people. You're going to like the forest."

The Merry Men, Charming, Snow White, and, finally, Mr. Canis left the shack. Canis turned back for one moment. "You say my name was Tobias Clay?"

Sabrina nodded.

"I'm very eager to get to know him," he said, then he was gone.

• • •

Nottingham dragged the family in for questioning, but after several hours he released them. Despite his anger he had no proof that anyone in the Grimm family had been responsible for freeing Canis, killing Bluebeard, or inciting the riot. Still, he made it clear that soon he would have all of them at the ends of nooses.

Uncle Jake dropped Briar Rose off at her coffee shop and promised to call later. She smiled and whispered something into his ear. He grinned like a child on Christmas morning and watched her walk away.

"What did she say?" Daphne asked.

"She said she is in love with me."

"Barf!" Puck cried.

When they pulled into the driveway, Sabrina was startled to see

Nurse Sprat standing on the front porch.

"Nurse Sprat," Granny cried when she got out of the car. "We're very sorry we're late. We were detained by the sheriff."

Nurse Sprat was finishing off a meatball sandwich and seemed quite content. "No problem, Mrs. Grimm. I hope you aren't in any trouble."

"Trouble is practically our middle name," Granny said.

"I brought the girl. She's around here somewhere—oh, here she comes," Sprat said, gesturing to the side of the house. There, Sabrina was shocked to see Red Riding Hood bounding around the corner with Elvis in tow.

"Is this your doggie?" Red asked. "He's so much fun."

Elvis licked the girl happily.

"What is she doing here?" Sabrina asked.

Granny knelt down to eye level with Red. "She's coming to stay with us."

"What!"

"Mr. Canis asked us to look after her while he's away, and I think it's a wonderful idea. Red needs some friends while she works on her memory."

Red smiled at the girls.

"But she tried to kill us," Sabrina said.

"Sabrina, don't hold a grudge."

Granny gave Red Mr. Canis's bedroom and promised that she would take the child shopping the next day for some more modern clothing. Sabrina followed her sister up to their room, tired as a dog, but Daphne did not enter the room. She went into Granny's and closed the door. It broke Sabrina's heart. Winning her sister's respect back was going to take a lot of work.

She went to bed, but without Daphne the room seemed huge and lonely. She tossed and turned, and though she was exhausted she couldn't sleep. After a while she decided to visit her parents. She opened the door and found them there, still soundly slumbering on the queen-size bed. She crawled in between them and closed her eyes. She heard Mirror clear his throat and knew his face had appeared in the reflection.

"Want to see where Goldilocks is?" he asked.

Sabrina fought back a tear. "No, we're done looking. She doesn't want to come back. Not that I can blame her really. If I could get out of this town I might never come back."

"I know exactly how you feel, Starfish," Mirror said.

Sabrina watched his face disappear. She reached over and kissed her father on the cheek, then did the same to her mother. Her kisses weren't magical. They wouldn't wake Henry and Veronica. But maybe they made a difference to her parents. They certainly made a difference to her. She closed her eyes and drifted to sleep.

Sometime in the night, Sabrina heard a knock on the door downstairs. She climbed out of bed and went down the steps, wondering who could be visiting at such a late hour. Perhaps it was Puck. He was known to forget his keys. Or maybe Red had decided to have a look around and had gotten locked out.

She reached for the doorknob with one hand and rubbed the sleep out of her eyes with the other. When she opened the door she gaped at what she saw. There were three enormous brown bears on the porch, one in a hat and tie, a second in a purple polka-dotted dress, and the third in a Cleveland Indians baseball cap. Two of the bears stood nearly eight feet tall, while the smallest was just a few inches over Sabrina's height.

Then a fourth person pushed her way to the front. She had freckles across her nose, a bronzed tan, big green eyes, and blond curls the color of precious metal.

"Goldilocks?" Sabrina gasped.

The woman nodded. "Sorry I'm late. I had to pick up a few friends. This town is dangerous, you know." Goldilocks smiled. "So, I hear someone in this house needs a kiss."

To be continued in

THE SISTERS GRIMM

BOOK SEVEN

THE EVERAFTER WAR

ABOUT THE AUTHOR

Michael Buckley is the *New York Times* bestselling author of the *Sisters Grimm* and *NERDS* series. He has also written and developed television shows for many networks. Michael lives in Brooklyn, New York, with his wife, Alison, and his son, Finn.

This book was designed by Melissa Arnst, and art directed by Chad W. Beckerman. It is set in Adobe Garamond, a typeface that is based on those created in the sixteenth century by Claude Garamond. Garamond modeled his typefaces on those created by Venetian printers at the end of the fifteenth century. The modern version used in this book was designed by Robert Slimbach, who studied Garamond's historic typefaces at the Plantin-Moretus Museum in Antwerp, Belgium.

The capital letters at the beginning of each chapter are set in Daylilies, designed by Judith Sutcliffe. She created the typeface by decorating Goudy Old Style capitals with lilies.

Enjoy this sneak peek at

THE EVERAFTER WAR

BOOK SEVEN IN THE *SISTERS GRIMM* SERIES

"This has been a stupid wild-goose chase!" Sabrina exclaimed. "The Master and the Scarlet Hand are probably getting a big laugh out of this right now!"

"Don't give up hope, Starfish," Mirror said.

"Give up hope! I haven't had any hope in two years."

"Bummer!" Puck said. "Well, maybe whoever is pounding on the door downstairs can wake your dad up."

"Puck, could you answer it for me?" Granny asked.

"What am I? The butler?"

"I'll get it," Sabrina said. She needed to get out of the room. The disappointment was hanging in the air, threatening to suffocate her.

"Freaking out isn't helping Mom and Dad," Daphne said as she raced down the stairs after Sabrina. "Exploding in frustration every time we have a setback is, well, annoying."

Sabrina marched to the door the turned to face her sister. "First of all, you don't even know the meaning of most of the words in that last sentence. I'll be angry and upset if I want. I have a right to be angry. My life is horrible."

Sabrina threw the door open and there, standing on the porch, was a rail-thin woman with a hooked beak of a nose and eyes like tiny black holes. She was dressed entirely in gray. Her handbag was gray. Her hair was gray. When she smiled, her teeth were gray.

"I think it's about to get a lot worse," Daphne groaned.

"Hello, girls," the woman said.

"Ms. Smirt!" Sabrina cried.

"Oh, you remember me. How it warms the heart," she said as she snatched them by the wrists and dragged them out of the house and across the lawn, where a taxicab was waiting in the driveway.

"Where are you taking us?" Daphne cried, trying and failing to break free from the woman's iron talons.

"Back to the orphanage," Smirt snapped. "You don't belong here. Your grandmother is unfit. She kidnapped you from your foster father."

Sabrina remembered the last foster father Smirt had sent them to live with. Mr. Greeley was a certifiable lunatic. "He was a serial killer. He attacked us with a crowbar."

"The father-child bond needs time to develop," Smirt said as she pushed the girls into the backseat of the taxi.

"You can't send us back to him," Daphne shouted.

"Sadly, you are correct. Mr. Greely is unavailable to take you back due to an unfortunate incarceration. But don't worry. I've already found you a new foster family. The father is an amateur knife thrower. He's eager for some new targets . . . I mean, daughters."

Smirt slammed the cab's door shut. She tossed a twenty-dollar bill at the driver. "You got automatic locks on this thing?"

Suddenly, the locks on the doors were set.

"To the train station, please," Smirt said. "And there's another twenty in it if you can make the 8:14 to Grand Central."

The taxi charged out of the driveway and tires squealed as it made a beeline toward the Ferryport Landing train station.

"You can't take us back to the orphanage," Sabrina said. "We're not orphans anymore. We found our mother and father."

"Such an imagination you have, Sophie," Smirt said. "There's really nothing as unattractive in a child as an imagination."

"My name is Sabrina!"

In no time, the taxi was pulling into the train station. Ms. Smirt pinched the girls on their shoulders and hustled them onto the waiting train. The doors closed before Sabrina and Daphne could make a run for it.

"Find a seat, girls," she said as the train rolled out of the station.

"Daphne, don't worry," Sabrina whispered as she took her sister's hand and helped her into a seat. Sabrina had many talents, but her greatest was the ability to devise effective escape plans. While she comforted her sister she studied the exit doors, windows, and even the emergency brake. A daring escape was already coming together when she noticed the complete lack of worry on her little sister's face.

"I've got this one covered," Daphne said.

"You what?" Sabrina asked.

The little girl put her palm into her mouth and bit down on it.

"What's going on, Daphne?" Sabrina continued, eyeing the girl suspiciously. Daphne had never plotted an escape. Escaping had been the exclusive domain of Sabrina Grimm for almost two years. What did her little sister have in mind?

"Zip it!" Ms. Smirt snapped before Daphne could explain. "I don't want to have to sit on this train for two hours with a couple of chatterboxes." The caseworker snatched a book out of her handbag and flipped it open. Sabrina peered at the title: *The Secret.*

"Ms. Smirt, have you ever heard of the Brothers Grimm?" Daphne said.

The caseworker scowled and set her book on her lap. "What do you want?"

"I was wondering if you have ever heard of the Brothers Grimm."

"They wrote the fairy tales," Ms. Smirt said.

Daphne shook her head. "That's what most people believe, but it's not true. The Brothers Grimm didn't write stories— they wrote down things that really happened. The fairy tales aren't made-up stories. They're warnings to the world about Everafters."

Sabrina was stunned. Daphne was spilling the family's secret to the worst possible person. They couldn't trust Smirt any further than they could throw her.

"What's an Everafter?" the caseworker snapped.

"It's what fairy-tale characters like to be called," the little girl explained. "'Fairy-tale character' is kind of a rude term. Like I was saying, the Brothers Grimm wrote about Everafters because they are real. Take Snow White. She's a real person and the story really happened—poison apple and all. Cinderella, Prince Charming, Beauty and the Beast, Robin Hood—they're all real people. They actually live here in Ferryport Landing. The Queen of Hearts is the mayor. Sleeping Beauty is dating our uncle."

"Debbie, you are going to look so adorable in your straitjacket," Ms. Smirt said.

"It's Daphne," the little girl said.

"Please be quiet," Sabrina whispered into her sister's ear.

"OK, kid, I'll bite. So, if fairy-tale characters are real, how come I haven't met any?" the caseworker said with a cackle.

"Because there's a magical barrier that surrounds this town that keeps the Everafters inside. Our great-great-great-great-grandfather Wilhelm Grimm and a witch named Baba Yaga built it to stop some evil Everafters from invading nearby towns."

"Oh, of course," Smirt said sarcastically. She slapped her knee and let out a ghastly laugh that sounded like a wounded moose. Sabrina had never seen the nasty woman laugh before and hoped she never would again.

Daphne ignored Smirt. "The barrier has made people in the town angry, and a lot of the Everafters don't like us much," Daphne said. "But—"

"Daphne, stop. You've told her too much," Sabrina begged.

"Let me finish, Sabrina," Daphne said calmly. "Like I was saying, we have a lot of enemies in Ferryport Landing. but we've managed to make a few friends."

Suddenly there was a tap on the window. Sabrina gazed out, expecting to see the Hudson River rushing past. Instead, what she saw nearly caused her to fall out of her seat. In the window was a familiar ragged-haired boy in cowboys-fighting-monkeys pajamas. Held aloft by two giant pink insect wings, he soared alongside the speeding train, grinning and sticking his tongue out at her. Sabrina had never been so happy to get a raspberry in her life.

To be continued . . .

Look for
THE COUNCIL OF MIRRORS,
the ninth book in the series!

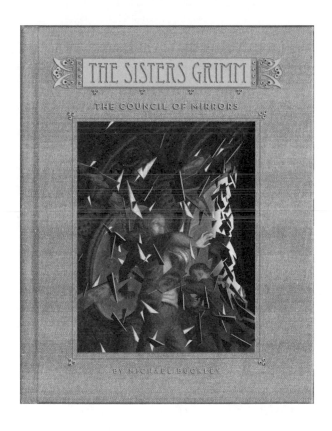

THE SISTERS GRIMM

Look for

A VERY GRIMM GUIDE

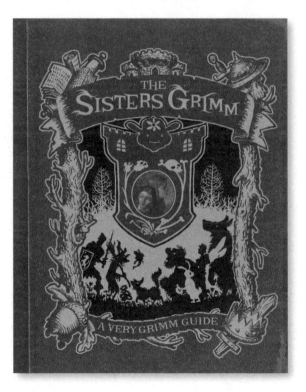

Inside information on your favorite
book series by Michael Buckley

THE SISTERS GRIMM

Catch the magic—

read all the books in Michael Buckley's *New York Times* bestselling series!

A Today Show Book Club Pick!

BOOK ONE:
THE FAIRY-TALE DETECTIVES

BOOK TWO:
THE UNUSUAL SUSPECTS

BOOK THREE:
THE PROBLEM CHILD

BOOK FOUR:
ONCE UPON A CRIME

BOOK FIVE:
MAGIC AND OTHER MISDEMEANORS

BOOK SIX:
TALES FROM THE HOOD

BOOK SEVEN:
THE EVERAFTER WAR

BOOK EIGHT:
THE INSIDE STORY

BOOK NINE:
THE COUNCIL OF MIRRORS

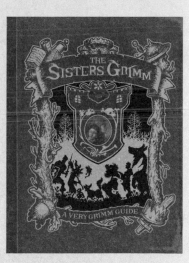

Read *A Very Grimm Guide*, available now!